ANTIPODES

Other Works in English by Ignacio Padilla

Shadow Without a Name

ANTIPODES
ANTIPODES

Ignacio Padilla

TRANSLATED BY ALASTAIR REID

Scribner

First published in Great Britain by Scribner, 2004
An imprint of Simon & Schuster UK Ltd
A Viacom Company

Originally published in 2001 by Espasa Calpe, Spain, as
Las Antípodas y el siglo

1 3 5 7 9 10 8 6 4 2

Simon & Schuster UK Ltd
Africa House
64–78 Kingsway
London WC2B 6AH

www.simonsays.co.uk

Simon & Schuster Australia
Sydney

A CIP catalogue record for this book is available from the British Library

ISBN 0-7432-3983-0

Printed and bound in Great Britain by
Mackays of Chatham plc, Chatham, Kent

To Indira and Pedro Ángel Palous,

fellow sailors on this boat

Contents

Contents

The Antipodes and the Century

For them, Edinburgh was not so much a name for somewhere else as a secret voice that invoked the blessed city that had been destined for them from the beginning of time. It also meant undergoing forty days and nights in the Ka-Shun Desert, lashing camels near to death. One after the other, men and animals would collapse exhausted on the dunes, gasping out a kind of prayer as they gave up the ghost—although no one could make out what language that wandering band had chosen to speak. All of a sudden, their eyes, dry now for so long from the wastes of stone and salt, filled once again with tears, in which Scotland's capital gleamed for a moment, a palace preserved in amber. It was as if someone had intruded into their retinas an elephantine fortress of streets, bridges, and windows which, like alien eyes from another century, would watch their own eyes close in final peace in their tombs of sand. Only then could the survivors leave behind their dead with their minds at ease, certain that both conquerors and conquered would find themselves again in the city that waited for them behind the Great Wall, where they could slake the dry thirst of the journey, to the sound of the bagpipes they had fashioned out of yak bladders, using old instruments for pipes.

Under the weight of so many deaths and such longings, little time remained to the wanderers to think of the days they had left behind. A faint remembrance of a delicate rooftop in Beijing, the feel of rice paddies on the knees, or the memory of an unsuspecting foreigner who, involved in preparations for his journey, had come over to ask of them where their caravan was headed. It amused them to recall how one of the guides, tight-lipped or timid, answered that question with a vague shrug, waving a hand toward the western peaks and muttering the arcane name of the city in such an unmistakable Scottish accent that the questioning foreigner was sure he had misheard. "Embruh," repeated the guide with a vague priestly gesture, before leaving abruptly, as though the mere mention of that name had acted like a spur to his side.

In reality, nobody had an exact idea in which meridian lay the city of such illusions. Not even the men who acted as caravan guides dared to go farther than a narrow pass on the horizon, a stony gash through which it was possible to make out a shimmering haze of towers that could well be a glassy mirage on the horizon. Those who went past the point disappeared once and for all, and if on some occasion even the guides let themselves be led astray by the travelers, there was no way of knowing in Beijing if the caravan had gone beyond the spur of stone, or if sun, thirst, and the tortures of sand had obliterated them on the journey, as we brush away a trail of insects. On such

occasions, they had to discover all over again the traces
of the city, decipher its location from the blind voices of
opium smokers or in the imprecise maps made on feverish
nights when a sated nomad let fall to a prostitute more
than he should have. Sometimes, however, the dark weight
of the secret or the intensity of those who held it could not
prevent some loudmouth from waking up in the common
stocks, silenced as a warning to any who were dreaming of
an opportune moment to set off in search of Edinburgh.
They say, too, that in Mongolia today ghostly stories circulate about a German Jesuit who in his letters to Rome
spoke of the existence of a kind of global map in the very
heart of the Gobi Desert, a vague though tangible diorama
of the cosmos, its center a replica of the Scottish capital.
But the voices tell also how that man, with his books and
his visions, was gone before anyone had been able to understand what he said. All in all, for the men of the Gobi,
their city was neither replica nor reflection of anywhere
else: it was the home, real and unique, that a divine messenger had ordered them to build half a century ago, when
for them the world was little more than an expanse of
dunes, kept alive by two feeble and cretaceous rivers.

They say, too, that in those days, far in the past by now,
that divine messenger bore the name of Donald Campbell.
He was the most distinguished member of the Geographical Society and had arrived in China too late to join the
legendary expedition of Younghusband. Perhaps it was the
vertigo of the desert or perhaps simply his sense of duty
that drove Campbell to take to the desert alone, nursing

the hope of one day catching up with the Briton who re-traced the steps of Marco Polo. But Younghusband never managed to meet his Scottish follower, for Campbell had not traveled more than a hundred miles when he was set upon by a patrol of Tibetan guards and left half dead in the dunes in a mess of blood. Nobody knows for how long or how fiercely that man wished for some wind from Scot-land while his skin and his brain were broiling under the sun. What is known is that, one fine afternoon, a tribe of Kirghiz nomads saved him from death, set his body astride a camel, and so led him to the beginning or the end of his unfortunate journey.

Certainly it was then that the Scottish engineer lost the blessing of forgetting, to a point where time and the cosmos fused in his hallucinations. Suddenly everything became for him a plan in which realities, wishful and ac-tual, alternated, and the shiftings of his disturbed memory neither could nor wanted to remain in the desert. In his sun-scorched mind, those who saved his life were not the Kirghiz but a battalion of grenadiers who had discovered his inert body in the sand, an army surgeon who had healed his wounds, and a naval vessel that had taken him and his men to his beloved Edinburgh. Initially, perhaps, the city in its details and the faces that greeted him in his family house in the Lawnmarket seemed hazy to him, as if the spires, their features, and even their speech were still contaminated by the unpleasant memories of China which kept troubling his feverish brain; or perhaps some morn-ing his sickroom seemed to be covered with pelts, while the waves of the North Sea sparkled for him with a sandy light, which he put down to the effects of his sojourn in the Gobi Desert. Campbell, however, was not long in returning to his university chair in Old College, and if at times the faces of his students startled him with their slanted eyes, he was soon able to convince himself that things would eventually resume their proper course, and that the desert would stay in his remembering only in the form of those teasings of memory which would end up seeming trivial to him, however appealing.

The Kirghiz, meanwhile, gave themselves over with great passion to deciphering the delirious voice of the prophet the desert had brought them. With the help of those who knew something of the world and its peoples on the other side of the Great Wall, the Kirghiz managed to transcribe his words one by one. With great care, they transferred them to wooden tablets, and they pored over them like scholars. Not until then did they dare to question Campbell, but only when they saw that he was distracted, wrapped in the all-embracing smile of those monks who seem never to wake from their dreaming. With some luck, after a few months, they were able to follow his instructions and carry out his wishes, in utter conviction that a blessed deity had chosen them to receive his designs from the Other Side. Later, when the divine messenger showed signs of a returning strength, they found for him a cedar board and pieces of black chalk, so that he might show them the shapes and measurements that previously in his tent he had traced in the air with the passion of a teacher lost in his fanciful lecture. So, little by little but inevitably, through a mixture of patience and devotion, they learned the exact height that Edinburgh Castle must attain, the precise length of the bridge that connects the High Street with Waverly Station, the correct calculations necessary to establish the perimeter of Canongate Cemetery, or the true distance between the two spires of St. Giles' Cathedral.

It was not many years before those drawings in the air began to take form among the rocks of the Gobi. The rumor that a divine voice was present in the desert drew a multitude of men and women who wished to dedicate their lives to building a vast sanctuary for a new religion, with a Templar-like liturgy in the form of measurements, azimuth lines, parabolas, and a whole host of topographical directions that the new inhabitants of Edinburgh had followed without thinking for various decades. Insatiable, devoted, they dug unceasingly in the sand; they shaped the rock as if it were just a question of helping the earth to become finally the place that had been taking shape deep within it for several centuries. Nothing drove them as much as the declining age of their prophet. Long had they waited for their moment of fulfillment, and in consequence their lives were filled with a cathedral-sized joy such as you find only in those races that have spent aeons in contemplating only the landscape. They were sure it would give them no trouble to learn later just how they should live and die in the city they were building. In time, in the same Canongate, they would burn three women heretics for their traffic in false dogma, they would drink malt beer from large ceramic mugs, and their children, heads full of elves and fairies, would end up detesting the English, although they dressed just like them and ended up speaking their language with a Caledonian cast; and they memorized the verses that Campbell, stirred by dreams of his students in Old College, would recite to them for evenings on end, gesticulating in the air with his left hand and putting into words the beginnings of the small universe that was taking shape for him in both stone and memory.

For forty years, Campbell had dispensed his knowledge in the halls of Architecture in Old College, fruitful years, no question, attached as he was to Edinburgh with the enthusiasm of someone who knows his words will not go wasted on the air, but will take on substance in the thousands of faces that passed before him in those years. Bit by bit, he gave up his Sunday habits and refused to be apart from his disciples, for he had discovered how much he loved them, how much he needed to speak with them, as a grounding for his mind, a distant mind that kept tricking him with nightmares and fantasies from the unfortunate wanderings of his youth in the deserts of China.

Finally, his body worn out with crisscrossing in his mind the map of his beginnings, he announced one morning that this day would be the last of his life. Campbell appeared in the halls of Old College and told his students that he wished to say goodbye to the sea. Hundreds of hands bore him reverently to the top of Calton Hill, and from there the old architect wept for joy at the sight of the waves of the North Sea. Meanwhile, his beloved followers were watching in the far distance a mounting pinnacle of whirling sand, the prelude to the storm that would ultimately level the century, burying it under a vast sand dune, mountainous and mute.

Chronicle of the Second Plague

The records of the second plague come down to no more than speculations—loose dates and contradicting theories that still circulate in the medical faculty of the University of Kent. Some of its more distinguished members seriously question the spread of the epidemic, but the majority concur in their view that Sir Richard de Veelt based his medical findings not on his observation of the epidemic itself but on another document of unknown origin, barely detectable in the notes the distinguished Crown Counselor forwarded to Europe some months before he disappeared.

Judging by the oblique nature of his notes, Sir Richard must have found that other notebook in some obscure corner of the St. Martin Mission, perhaps blurred and damaged by the humidity of the Amazon, perhaps at the mercy of termites in the ruins of a chapel. There was no important heading that might have given the celebrated explorer some idea of what was in those incomplete pages, nor had anyone taken the trouble to hide them in a strongbox. To whom would they have mattered, these pages? What would anyone who did not have de Veelt's knowledge have made of the hundreds of normal cardiograms, the records of glucose in perfect equilibrium, blood pressures enviably level? To establish its very existence, what that anonymous report revealed came precisely from what was not said, or, as de Veelt himself suggests, in the utter disregard shown by the victims of the second plague toward their invisible infection. Truly, no man in his right mind could have perceived an illness in so asymptomatic an appearance, an illness the first sign of which was perfect health. If you add that this particular epidemic struck St. Martin in the wake of a fierce outbreak of bubonic plague, it is no wonder that the contrast alone led sufferers and doctors alike to consider the second plague as a blessing rather than as the onset of a new epidemic even more destructive than death.

It is difficult to imagine just how much time de Veelt was able to spend with these pages, or what he managed to glean from them. Perhaps he had them for a few hours, enough to discover with some dread that he had contracted the disease and that his habitual infirmities had completely disappeared. He ought then to have consigned these notes to the cemetery of neutral texts, as out of sight as the sickness they identify. Perhaps later the counselor wondered if the substance of that record, so neat and perfect, had raised the same alarms in the inquiring spirit of some missionary, or in the mind of whoever, ages before, had written them down just as he had now read them—terrified, dwelling in this jungle retreat on the ironies of so macabre a god, who had relieved St. Martin of the bubonic plague only to visit on his creatures a second epidemic more in keeping with his sinister personal clock.

How could anyone have made this clear to the inhabitants of St. Martin, while they were rejoicing in their new health as a well-deserved miracle? The fact that these people had survived the ravages of bubonic plague left them with the firm conviction that they had paid up the quota of pain that divine providence exacts from each person, each place. When the second plague began to make its presence felt, there was a death in every dwelling, a hanging smell of burning flesh, and a solid carpet of rats as big as dogs waiting for their own cremation in the atrium of the church. In Sir Richard's considered opinion, scenes of that nature must have at least stimulated the native population with a will to live beyond their natural limits, and in that way the cruel memory of past pain seemed reason enough for them to believe that the sores, the tears, and the yellow vomit had immunized them against death, as happens when viruses carry vaccines for other infections. In that way, unable to understand their own helplessness and given to disobeying the laws of nature, the people of St. Martin had chosen to ignore death, or, as the counselor suggests, quoting his hypothetical notebook, to assimilate it with a superhuman vitality.

Even so, it would be wrong to charge the public health authority with negligence for having suspected nothing when the hospital, formerly packed with the sick and the dying, suddenly emptied dramatically and reassuringly. Now we know from other sources that the colonial government at one point saw the hospital desertion as a logical reaction on the part of the people to the increased charges levied by the medical services during the bubonic plague. But Sir Richard's notes do not go in for such speculation—his attention is more taken up with the astonishing results obtained by the notebook's author when he examined certain victims of the disease. There is a note on how cirrhotic livers continued to function perfectly, how bodies had ceased to register infection, and how minds had come to reject utterly notions of pain and death. De Veelt acknowledges having read in the notes a record of hundreds of similar instances, in which the writer has tested patients' extremities with a scalpel, or has struck them to the point of drawing blood, without seeing any alteration in their fundamental good humor. Either from timidity or from extreme skepticism, the investigator had finally to admit his complete impotence when confronting these desperate and mutilated bodies, or in seeing flame applied to the flesh of those who showed the same indifference to their wounds as someone listening to an incomprehensible foreign language.

Sir Richard's comments in the latter part of the notebook are extremely laconic. It is difficult besides to separate from them his vision of a St. Martin turned into a kind of leper colony whose abandoned and deformed inhabitants began one day to conceive of an infirmity that would restore them to life. About that time, the patients would take to mutilating themselves, and wandering among the disintegrating buildings of the mission. In the end, their bodies, already embarked on a process of slow but inevitable disintegration, would have accepted a kind of life that was fragmented and infected, but nevertheless would retain sufficient vitality to devour Sir Richard de Veelt while he was reading the last pages of the notebook, in the certainty that one day the particles of his physical body, still squirming with life, would be dispersed by the wind that blew from the Amazon.

Ever Wrest: Log of the Journey

Maurice Wilson came up with the idea of conquering Everest while in hospital on the outskirts of Munich, dying of tuberculosis. He knew that his abilities then as a mountaineer were no more than average, but he was sure that his plan for conquering the mystical summit required only a little patience and a dash of good luck. His idea could not be simpler, as he once wrote to his mother: after driving off his tuberculosis with a strict regimen of meditation and a vegetarian diet, he would take flying lessons and bring down his plane as high as possible on the mountain. As for the rest of the ascent, it would not prove too difficult, if he had some practice in the Lake District and got back the fine physical condition that had brought him the Military Cross in the past for his action in the Third Battle of Ypres.

Days before coming to this decision, Wilson had read in the newspapers of the failure of George Mallory and Andrew Irvine on the edge of the so-called Third Base Camp, scarcely three hundred meters from the summit. Turned overnight into heroes and martyrs of the British

Empire, the names of both climbers assumed an aura of sanctity on everyone's lips, which to Wilson, who had been cashiered from the Army for stealing a woman's dress from a store in New Zealand, could only seem excessive. There was no doubt in his mind that these two young gentlemen from Cambridge had thrown their lives away by following the wrong route. No one could blame them for wanting to surmount the highest peak in the world, but, with the greatest respect, it is the height of foolishness to devote more time and effort to that doomed enterprise than the available minimum. The endless snows of Everest, with no buried treasure, no enemy to conquer other than the cold and the altitude, could easily give shelter to all kinds of idiots, but at least Wilson planned to enter history as the most practical and realistic of them, and perhaps for that reason destiny might reward him with an immortality the absurdity of which made it no less desirable.

Convinced then of the utter feasibility of his project, Wilson lost no time in surprising his doctors with a recovery worthy of better motives. As a sick man, he not only refused the help volunteered by the Bavarian sanitarium but called into serious question the most modern treatments by gracefully overcoming his infirmity through prayer, bizarre sexual exercises, a prolonged sleep, and the ample ingestion of a ghastly bouillabaisse which he prepared, on his mother's instructions, with sugar, carrots, and a pinch of thyme. As soon as he was discharged, Wilson sent to a London editor a short paper with the title "How I Beat the Khoh Bacillus," in which he revealed that he

owed his amazing self-cure not just to his mother's culi-
nary wisdom but also to a rigorous mental control of the
pituitary gland and the subsequent intensification of the
libido. No physician or scientific academy ever dared to at-
test to the singular methods of Maurice Wilson, but the
relative commercial success of that paper at least made it
possible for its author to underwrite the cost of a secondhand Gypsy Moth, which he rechristened, suggestively,
Ever Wrest.

The papers of the day insist that Maurice Wilson left
behind at the London Aero Club a balance of two injured
instructors, with another hospitalized in Hull suffering a
nervous breakdown. Even so, after four weeks, his iron will
and his general good cheer brought him a second-class flying license, quite enough to set him off on his journey
without attracting the attention of the authorities.

After a brief spell of physical conditioning among the
peaks of the Lake District, Wilson set out in early April
on course for Bradford, where he planned to say goodbye
to his mother before setting out for Tibet. Unfortunately,
the *Ever Wrest* began to lose altitude soon after taking off,
and Wilson had to make an emergency landing on the
roof of a farm in Yorkshire. The accident did little to
change his plans, although it brought him more publicity
than he would have liked. Informed by the press of his
proposed wanderings in Nepalese air space, along with a
long record of his sexual excesses during his Army career,
the Air Ministry wasted no time in imposing an absolute
ban on any flights of his beyond the English Channel.

Wilson, however, ignored their warning, repaired the *Ever Wrest* in less than three weeks, and took off from Stag Lane on a foggy morning in May.

Among the many omissions in the British records of this affair, what catches the attention is that none of them gives credit to Maurice Wilson for having flown solo the eight thousand kilometers between Great Britain and the India of the Raj. Add to that the numerous attempts of the authorities to thwart him, refusing him permission to land in Cairo and Bahrain, and there is no doubt that he deserved to be mentioned alongside Ribbentrop and Amelia Earhart. However it happened, the fact is that *Ever Wrest* unquestionably made the flight to India, where Wilson had no alternative but to land. Forced to surrender his valiant plane to the indignant representatives of the Air Ministry, Wilson wrote a mournful letter to his mother in which he once again rejected both British law and the cardboard heroes of his boyhood, whose only merit according to him was to let themselves be led even to death by the indecipherable whims of a power that was now conspiring against him and his visionary schemes, to put them in their place, once and for all.

How Wilson managed to remain at liberty and besides that to receive compensation for the seizing of *Ever Wrest* still puzzles his biographers. Anyone else in his place would have ended up a bag of bones in a Delhi prison, no question, or, at best, on the first boat back to London. But Wilson was cut from a different cloth—he knew very well that all laws, natural and human, had been put in his path only to provide him with the pleasure of breaking them. Consequently, as soon as he received his compensatory £500, he once again brushed aside the order he had been given not to set foot in Nepal, signed up three experienced porters, and arrived with them at the Rongbuk Monastery in the record time of twenty-five days.

Maurice Wilson's stay in the monastery of Rongbuk is recorded in the early pages of a diary found a year later among his belongings. Once again committed to prayer and to his odd diet of thyme and carrots, the climber here describes his first encounter with the magnificence of the Himalayan glaciers, and announces to his unlikely readers his new proposal: he will say nothing to anyone about whether or not he reaches the summit of Everest. Uncertainty and anonymity, Wilson claims in his sketchy travel notes, would surely be the best offerings a man like himself could leave as his revenge on posterity and on the false heroics of those who might follow in his footsteps. At this present time, it is impossible to know if Wilson was in a position to bring off an enterprise like this; but it is reasonable to suspect that in the face of such a curious challenge, the official versions of Wilson's last days differ dramatically from those framed by legend or by speculative biographical reconstruction.

If we go by British accounts of Wilson's ascent, we are led to think that he first attacked the mountain in mid-April. Some days later, cold and inexperience forced him to return to the monastery, only to plan a new attempt in the middle of May, this time with his porters, who, however, refused to go with him any farther than the last camp. It was there, they say, that Wilson broke with his stoical habits and devoured five cans of provisions from Fortnum & Mason, left in the camp the previous year by a British expedition. Alone and satiated, Wilson had then tried to climb the North Coll, until he ran into a massive wall of ice where, after first writing in his diary that the next day, after exercising his pituitary gland, he would again attempt the conquest of the summit, he died. There he was found a year later by the expedition led by Eric Shipton, who wrapped the frozen body of Wilson the adventurer in the remains of his tent, later to commit it to the eastern arm of the Rongbuk, in the hope that the ice of the glacier might wipe out all trace of his legendary pigheadedness.

Nothing else is known with any certainty about the last days of Maurice Wilson. For years, British alpinists have insisted on telling raucous versions—that Eric Shipton had found the poor devil's body wearing a woman's dress, that Edmund Hillary himself kept in his London house a much-prized second log of the journey, in which his predecessor had noted his wildest sexual fantasies. There is little chance of confirming anything in that document; but the fiction of Wilson wearing women's clothes does have a sequel somewhat disturbing in the annals of British mountaineering. Apparently true to the persistence that had characterized his whole life, the body of the unfortunate climber turned up regularly in the Rongbuk Glacier, until a Chinese party rescued it from its icy tomb in 1975.

An odd report, sent out at the time by a press agency in Peking, declares that Maurice Wilson did not die from exposure to cold but from asphyxiation, when he attempted to swallow a page from his diary in which he described in detail how he had conquered the longed-for summit of Everest. The Chinese say nothing about how Wilson's body was clothed; but it is still possible to view, in the Alpine Museum of the Communist Party, a voluptuous high-heeled shoe that the legendary mountaineer Chu Ying-hua swears he found under the snow only a few paces from the British flag that Sir Edmund Hillary planted on the summit of Everest just a few days before Princess Elizabeth was crowned in Westminster Abbey.

Ballistics: Some Notes

There is no denying that the craftsmen of Cappadocia were extremely accomplished, but anyone with half an eye could recognize an authentic Hutchinson–Van Neuvel among the many pirated copies that have shown up in the armies of Europe over the last five years. For a start, the butt of the Hutchinson, almost always carved from Fijian red oak, weighs exactly 3 pounds, 25 ounces, and measures 15.4 inches from stock to firing pin. In fact, it might be slightly shorter, but that depends more on the atmospheric conditions of warfare, not on Hutchinson's manufacturing practices. The weapon's weight, on the other hand, was always kept mathematically precise, truly one of its principal features: for even if the wooden stock of a counterfeit rifle expands much less in varying temperatures, Turkish oak is much more porous, which means that it will absorb large quantities of water, which increases the weapon's weight, with serious consequences not just where its accuracy is concerned but also on the body and endurance of the marksman. On repeated occasions, it has been possible to prove that if an average infantryman armed with an authentic Hutchinson–Van Neuvel were to fire for three hours at a rate of fifteen shots a minute, the skin area on his shoulder would end up with a bruise the size of a lemon, while in the case of a counterfeit weapon, particularly the Turkish version of '14, or even the Japanese model of '17, a soldier firing in identical circumstances would end up fracturing his collarbone. And, besides that, only 20 percent of his shots would have hit the target.

Take a hypothetical sniper who has to spend a long spell of time crouched down with a Hutchinson ready at his shoulder. Clearly, even when this man does not fire at all, the length of time and the sluggishness of blood circulation increase the weight of the weapon exponentially, causing serious pain in his shoulder. To date, we have no information as to how long the average rifleman could tolerate that pain with a fake Hutchinson as opposed to a genuine one; but speculation suggests that the time difference in bearing the weight of these two weapons could easily add up to months, even years.

Obviously, no ordinary man would ever agree to spend so much time on watch, but it is not beyond the imagination to understand how vastly the Hutchinson differs in so many respects from its imitations, however identical they may appear. Imagine a soldier, loyal, and well trained as a sentry to spend years of service on a watchtower, in a firing position. Imagine, too, that he has finally put out of his mind all the other necessities of life, and has transformed himself into a weapon as concentrated and as durable as his Hutchinson. This imaginary soldier is by now a machine, resistant, able to survive not just bad weather but the average duration of our most recent wars. Perhaps he has become fused with his own weapon, perhaps constant detonations have left him so deaf as not to hear the retreat called, perhaps he is so fixated on a specific target in the enemy trenches that he has not even noticed the cease-fire at the foot of his watchtower. In such a case, speculations surrounding the Hutchinson are not so much about weight as about many of its other characteristics.

It should be made clear at this point that the telescopic sight on the Hutchinson, the imitations as well as the genuine, has an extremely narrow radius of sight compared to more sophisticated firearms. That limitation, however, is due not to any flaw in its manufacture but rather to the fact that the precision of a telescopic sight is always inversely proportional to the width of the terrain it encompasses. It would be quite enough for our soldier-machine to have in his sights the other marksman on the enemy side for the rest of the landscape to disappear completely from his field of vision. In such circumstances, it would seem not improbable that such a sniper, cut off from sounds and crouched in a watchtower three meters high, sees nothing besides what he is aiming at. His world has shrunk to a span of some four meters, his mind takes in that small surface. He does not even see his enemy's whole body, only the millimetric distance between helmet and eyes, the space between the eyebrows where his shot must hit to bring his enemy down from his tower and leave him lifeless in the mud. Strictly speaking, the accuracy of the

Hutchinson telescopic sight would be enough in such circumstances for our sniper to destroy the enemy with a single shot, whenever the said target was not more than 800 yards away, in the case of the Hutchinson, or 780 yards, in the case of the Turkish or Japanese imitations.

But what would happen if the enemy marksman were in all respects identical to our hypothetical sniper, something like a ghostly reproduction of him, waiting, crouched down in a watchtower, and also armed with a Hutchinson–Van Neuvel? In this kind of speculation, ballistics lose their customary precision and we have to turn to psychology or even metaphysics to have a complete grasp of the circumstances.

The first dilemma that must be faced by our imaginary marksman, who has an apparently identical figure squarely in his sights, is his realization that his enemy holds him similarly in *his* sights, and that consequently they are each cast in the double role of killer and victim. From a humane perspective, if he were to see his situation in this light, he would fail in his duty and would refrain from firing at his mirror image. But, as we have said, the stark telescopic sight of the Hutchinson both fragments and objectifies the marksmen, turning them into mere killing machines. Their humanity is considerably diminished; their only aim becomes the annihilation of the enemy at the least possible cost. In a word, the ideal sniper would be one who has managed to shed all trace of emotion—his dreams of going home, the faces of those expecting him, also his debt

to his country. Of course, it would seem inevitable that, to
a mind so mechanized, there must occur the ironic notion
that, were our sniper to think of withdrawing, or reaching
for his trigger, he would instantly draw a shot from his
mirror sniper, who, like him, remains ready to fire at his
enemy's slightest movement. In this case, our hypothetical
crack shot would seem doomed to dwell eternally on the
probabilities of killing and being killed, a very difficult
consideration indeed, somewhat beyond the simple will
to survive, and one that forces us back relentlessly to con-
sidering the physical qualities of the Hutchinson–Van
Neuvel.

Let us take for a start the question of distance. If the
enemy were exactly 800 yards from our sniper, and armed,
just as he was, with a genuine Hutchinson, then their
shots, were they to fire in unison, would shatter one another in midair. But if one of the adversaries was armed
with a Hutchinson of Turkish manufacture, then the one
with the authentic model would prevail.

It is well known that our soldiers are better trained
than most at telling distances between themselves and
their targets; but they also know that 50 percent of our
Hutchinsons are of Turkish manufacture, while only
20 percent of the enemy rifles come from Cappadocia
or Okinawa. This appears in principle to put our troops at
a great disadvantage: specifically, our imaginary sniper,
who must know the statistics but is incapable of distin-
guishing an authentic Hutchinson from an imitation. This
man knows that the mathematical probabilities of his hit-

ting his target are less than his opponent's, and he understands that if he fires, and draws the fire of the other, his terror of dying without killing must be greater than that of his enemy. Luckily, we know on the other hand that the enemy soldiers are much less expert at judging distance and, besides that, are unaware of that particular statistic, firmly believing that it is our Army that has a greater percentage of the genuine Hutchinsons. For that reason, even when the real facts are against our side, the doubts of both snipers about the authenticity of their own rifles leave them both on the same level of uncertainty, to put it one way, and therefore of vulnerability.

In such circumstances, the marksmen, caught up in the same distress, the same uncertainty over the range and accuracy of their weapons, would have to face three alternatives: one, killing the enemy and surviving his shot unhurt; two, missing with a shot from his counterfeit Hutchinson and then dying from a bullet from his enemy's genuine model; three, witnessing the collision of the two identical bullets at some point above the battlefield.

In this speculative exercise, however, there is a fourth possibility, one that is outrageous and anathematical to the art of warfare: it is that both soldiers, hypothetical and identical, remain fixed indefinitely at their posts, each hoping that the other either retreats or fires. If we remember that our sentry has turned himself into a machine capable of such feats, this would surely result in our troops, returning to the trenches for a new war, coming upon the demoralizing spectacle of two paralyzed snipers or, in the worst of cases, the scattered pieces of two riflemen so old that their weakened bodies could not have withstood the recoil of their weapons when they fired, after so many years of hesitation. This odd kind of suicide seems a long way from the dilemma we are discussing, but it is still closely related to the question that plagued both men in waiting so long to fire their fatal shot. It concerns the importance of providing our troops with authentic Hutchinson–Van Neuvels, or at least of teaching them to distinguish the genuine ones from their imitations.

Rhodesia Express

Of the five officers who survived the Zambezi campaign, only Colonel Richard L. Eyengton remained troubled enough by it to return eventually to Salisbury. Although old and enfeebled by malaria, Eyengton not only readily accepted an invitation to take charge of Rhodesian Railways—he even swore that if in three months his trains were not running on time as infallibly as they did on the London-York line, he would shoot himself in the smoking room of the Hotel Prince Albert. Of course, there were plenty in the city who took that challenge as the obsession of an old man, but nobody dared to question the word of one who seemed ready to do anything at all to pay his debt to that country that had cost the British Army so much blood.

It took Colonel Eyengton exactly one month, a month of insults, disciplinary punishments, and extravagant bribes, to have his trains emulating English ones with dignity. For a time, the colonial newspapers went out of their way to praise the old soldier, setting him up as an example to younger generations. To all of that the colonel responded with a smile that was both reserved and complacent, but which finally was the honey of a revenge nurtured during the unspeakable nights of hardship, mosquitoes, and weeds that had marked his African youth.

But the novelty so easily achieved by the old officer would not linger long on the palate, for just two weeks before his sacrificial date, the train from Lusaka to Salisbury began to register delays of between five and ten minutes. Nothing at all was able to explain so dramatic an irregularity: the trains left the Lusaka station on time and crossed the Zambezi at full speed, to arrive infallibly late at their destination. On various occasions Eyengton himself took the trip, in locomotives at full steam; and more than once he joined the native gangs shoveling coal into the congested boilers. And always, he was enraged to find on the platform in Salisbury a crowd of gloved gentlemen and ladies with parasols who, murmuring and giggling, waved their watches as if enclosed in them lay the fatal mechanism that would soon oblige the director of Rhodesian Railways to cut off his own head. In these moments, the colonel was disposed to hate every single inhabitant in the city, but his sense of honor and his secret realization that he would have behaved in just the same way obliged him to bow gracefully from the window of his locomotive.

Finally, unable to resolve or even explain that portent in the appointed time, Eyengton had no recourse but to wait for the fatal day with the dignity expected of a gentleman. So, while the owners of the Prince Albert Hotel were sending out invitations for the gala dinner at which the old soldier was to honor his promise, he confined himself to settling his gambling debts, drawing up his will, and immersing himself every evening in the British railway timetables the *Southern Rhodesia Standard* continued to publish, uselessly and somewhat sarcastically.

That is how things stood, until one morning there appeared in the station office one Malachi Rice, a sergeant in the Fifth Battalion of Foot from Belfast. Himself a native of Holyhead, Colonel Eyengton was particularly suspicious of everything that came across from Irish soil, so that the mere appearance of such a visitor at such an edgy time seemed to him in the worst of taste, and he refused to see him. The sergeant, however, would not be intimidated by the old man's rejection, and such was his insistence that Eyengton finally agreed to hear what he had to say on condition that it be as short as the rule of Mary, Queen of Scots.

When he entered the office the sergeant announced himself with a military clicking of heels, and immediately went on to state with clipped precision the point of his visit: he said he knew the reasons for the delays on the Lusaka-Salisbury line, and he could immediately explain them if the colonel would grant him two hours of his time.

Eyengton seemed skeptical at the beginning. Apart from his rank, the sergeant seemed common to him, of the worst type—even his uniform looked awkward. He knew too many soldiers like Rice—square pegs, grumbling drunks, vultures who preyed on British honor, from whom nothing good could be expected. Even so, it was better to be prudent with such men. If Rice wanted to make a fool of him, it would be best to listen to him, catch him out, and then have some fun at his expense.

"Be so good as to explain yourself," Eyengton at last replied, waving the Irishman into a chair. But Rice remained standing, and after a moment of hesitation, he told the colonel they must first walk to the Nyasa Hospital, on the edge of the city.

"The hospital?" asked the old man indignantly. "What have I missed at the hospital, Sergeant?"

"Nothing, sir," replied Rice. "Let's say it's just a matter of demonstrating to you that you are doomed to arrive late wherever you go in Salisbury"—and so saying, he took a watch from his tunic, announced that it was precisely 11:45, and asked the colonel as they left to verify the time on his own watch.

Somewhat surprised, Eyengton obeyed Rice's instructions at once. It was obvious the man was mad, but something about him compelled obedience. Did Rice want to lead him to hell? Well then, get on with it, devil take it all.

The walk to Nyasa Hospital was sheer torture for Colonel Eyengton. Like most distances in Salisbury, the way was short enough, but the noon sun, the uphill slope of Victoria Street, and the hollow gaze of the gibbons made it into a real odyssey. To top it all, Sergeant Rice walked much too fast, as if hurrying to meet an imaginary friend. Dripping with sweat, feeling his age, the colonel could hardly keep up, his original curiosity evaporating with this stupid adventure that could only come, he was sure, to the worst of ends.

Reaching the hospital, Rice stopped, took out his watch, and made the announcement: "Five minutes past twelve, Colonel. Twenty minutes from your office to here."

With little energy left for confronting his guide, the old man confirmed the time. "And so, Sergeant," he said with some irony. "What does that prove?"

To which Sergeant Rice, perspiring and looking as exhausted as Eyengton, answered that for now he could prove nothing. It was imperative that they both walk back at once to the colonel's office.

"What kind of nonsense is this? If you plan to end my life prematurely, Sergeant, I still have the power to deal with a miserable Irishman."

Sergeant Rice took this reprimand with ill-concealed distress. It was clear that he was only too aware of the oddness of his demands and the risk he was taking in putting poor Colonel Eyengton through his test. He assured the colonel in all sincerity that it was no joke, and added that if Colonel Eyengton were not entirely satisfied with his explanation, he would shoot himself in the smoking room at the Prince Albert Hotel. Mollified by that promise, Eyengton agreed to follow through with the sergeant's plan.

So they set off. In a gesture of respect, Sergeant Rice had offered to carry the colonel's jacket—he himself had shed his tunic to ease their progress through the scorching streets. The African sun assailed them once again, the fury of its glare amplified by that of the curious crowds that had gathered at the corner of New Notting Hill and Victoria Street, drawn by rumors of the strange perambulations of these men in shirtsleeves, to jeer or cheer them on.

No sooner had they arrived back at their point of departure than Sergeant Rice went through the ritual of the watch and announced, "Thirty minutes, Colonel, sir, on the dot." Puzzled, Eyengton consulted his watch: a quarter to one.

"Surely a mistake," he muttered, hoping for some logical solution. But Sergeant Rice grinned as if he had just squared the circle, and looked at the old man as if that simple difference between the two times were enough to explain why the Lusaka-Salisbury train arrived late. Rice raised his hand, pointed importantly to the clock in the plaza, and declared, "Colonel, it is actually almost twelve thirty-five. It was our watches that were late in arriving."

Soon after that, Malachi Rice and Colonel Richard L. Eyengton were drinking a beer together on the terrace of a café in Mashonaland. By now, the old soldier had given up all resistance and listened to the Irish trooper as to the voice of an oracle, terrifying in its illumination. Rice had now grown hesitant. He looked out at the streets of Salisbury and spoke sparely, aware that he was removing from the colonel's whole existence an invisible but essential support. Then, realizing that it was already too late to stop, he continued, "Colonel, the natives here have a name for a strange affliction that seems only to affect settlers. They called it *nkalo*, and I'm afraid that, thanks to you, it has become an epidemic in Salisbury."

The colonel nodded, although he seemed not to have heard the sergeant. Sweat had dried on his wrinkled forehead in such a way as to make him look much older and more troubled. He swallowed hard, and muttered a curse that was not addressed to Rice but directed somewhere deep in the streets of the city.

"How dare they? How could a whole city deceive me like that?"

"In our language here," Rice went on, "the word *nkalo* means boredom or spleen. And it's not every day that a British officer blows his brains out in the smoking room of the Prince Albert."

There was silence for the space of several minutes. Colonel Eyengton sat stiffly in his chair until a spasm of fury shook his whole body and his voice sounded like the burbling of a spring deep in a cave: "But my watch, too, showed that we were late."

Rice, adjusting his watch, answered respectfully: "Forgive me, Colonel, but some military men when they retire keep the bad habit of removing their tunic whenever possible. No civilian approves of that; but it makes it much easier for any manipulators or even one of their servants to . . ."

The colonel gazed into the distance until his face recovered its customary gravity. Finally he sighed, stood up, clicked his heels, and thanked the trooper sincerely for his valuable information.

"I hope to see you at the Prince Albert, Sergeant," he said in his official voice.

"But will you not do something?" Rice asked. "After all, your trains always arrived on time."

Eyengton, wearily replacing his chair, replied simply: "So you have told me only too plainly, my friend. But there are other faults for which a gentleman does not deserve the forgiveness of a city."

So saying, with a firm and decisive step, he disappeared into the streets of Salisbury.

Darjeeling

Kintup must have been the worst tailor in the whole Raj when I called on him in his shop in Darjeeling. His long years on the shores of the Tsangpo had left him practically blind, and his hands, long deformed by Himalayan gangrene, made it hard to believe he could manage to thread a rope through a ship's eyebolt. That an old man in these circumstances had chosen such a profession to sustain his declining years seemed at first not only paradoxical but positively cruel. As Colonel Bailey had explained to me just before dispatching me to Darjeeling, Kintup had done more for the mapping of Asia than any other individual in our time. When I saw him, however, anyone in my place would have taken him only as a namesake of the legendary explorer and authority whose reputation Bailey was obsessed with restoring. Like a child lost in his empty workshop, shipwrecked among bobbins of thread, bolts of false tweed, and secondhand mannequins, Kintup seemed more than anything a ghostly re-creation of the most sedentary of beings. Were it not for his blindness or his weathered skin, no one would guess that he had spent the best years of his life measuring, looking for new paths, traveling with nothing in mind but to throw five hundred marked logs into a river the existence of which in these years was not even entered with any certainty in the archives of the Royal Geographical Society. The colonel had already given me some idea of certain strategies that in early days would have justified these apparently useless enterprises, but with time, I began to realize that, in fact, those pretexts had never been the real driving force in the man who years later would receive me in Darjeeling with indifference rather than ill will.

Colonel Bailey seemed not at all upset when I returned to Bombay with the news that Kintup had refused the thousand rupees Bailey had offered him as compensation for the trials of his younger days. This disconcerted me. While I was describing the circumstances in which I had found the old pundit, the colonel's face gradually changed until his features took on a boyish brightness as he followed my account. A few months previously, while we were traveling in the territories that Kintup had explored and recorded in his odyssey more than thirty years earlier, the colonel had revealed that his admiration for the old pundit was mixed with a secret loathing for the Royal Geographical Society, which had never recognized his worth. Now, however, as I described my visit to Darjeeling, it seemed that his admiration for the old tailor had become pure and absolute, free of resentment or rancor. In a way that I was then not quite able to grasp, Kintup's refusal of money from his former employer and his insistence on continuing to live in squalor had elevated his image in the colonel's mind to that of a divinity, part epic, part maternal, that men like Bailey spend years pursuing, with the sad realization that it must remain unattainable. As Bailey would tell me later, on the ship that carried us to London, heroes in our time are unpardonably doomed to be almost absurd figures. While it was clear at that moment that my superior was once more thinking about Kintup, I repeat that only now, some twenty years after my visit to the tailor in Darjeeling, have I come to understand the full meaning of his words.

Colonel Bailey left me little time to discover just why my meeting with Kintup had so perturbed him. During our crossing of the continent, his obsession with knowing all the details of the wretched state of the tailor or the few words he had addressed to me in declining his overdue reward hardly left me time to introduce into our conversation the few questions that remained hanging in the air. It was soon obvious that Bailey had no inclination to satisfy my curiosity, even less to explain why I was in his company other than for what I could tell him about my meeting in Darjeeling. It was as if my meeting with Kintup had at last given him a pretext for bringing to an end a journey that had lasted him all his life.

Perhaps that was why his body, accustomed in previous years to conducting brilliant military campaigns and prodigious feats of mountaineering, gradually drifted into disuse, until all that remained of him was a heap of wasted flesh that would never set foot on London docks. Just before he surrendered himself to death, however, the colonel summoned me to his cabin, and after making me describe once more my meeting with Kintup, he gripped my arm and let out a snort of laughter that seemed to come from the other side of death. "That pundit!" he exclaimed. "That pundit is the biggest son of a bitch in all creation!" And so saying, he gave up his soul to the devil in a mixture of delight and sarcasm which even today I find quite enviable.

Never in my life have I witnessed a funeral as lavish as that with which the Royal Geographical Society arranged to honor Colonel Eric Bailey. A gold medal gleamed on top of his coffin during the wake, the newspapers detailed his many military achievements, and his heirs received a pension for all his work as a cartographer, the amount of which made the thousand rupees refused by Kintup seem like a mere bagatelle. As for me, at another time I would most likely have felt some pride about the part I played in these events, but the truth is that at those levels I could not avoid the uneasy feeling that my former chief was insulting me from his niche in Westminster Abbey. Remembering his last words and the details, gone over a thousand times, of my meeting with the tailor in Darjeeling, I was tormented by the thought that there was some message in them that only they and I would be able to decipher. At various times I tried to remember for myself the guru's words, but all I could dredge up from my memory was Kintup's exasperating indifference, almost as if he were mocking my efforts to make him accept the thousand rupees that Colonel Bailey was sending him. It was at that

time that the Royal Geographical Society pressed me to
continue the work, both cartographic and military, of my
late chief in Nepal, an offer that I surprised myself by accepting, not at all with the intention of someday meriting
a funeral like the colonel's, but rather with the notion that
in that post I could finally obliterate my existence and
launch out on an odyssey of my own, as wild, or wilder,
than that of Kintup.

In the eyes of my superiors, the months in which I put
off going back to India were largely wasted. On the pretext
of studying in advance the maps that my chief had drawn
with the help of Kintup's earliest notes, I delayed my departure for some time, bent on digging up records that
might give me a more complete sense of the ill-fated story
of the pundit. There was little in the archives that had not
already passed through Bailey's hands: recruited in 1866 for
the Great Trigonometrical Survey of India, Kintup had
been sent to Nepal with the job of finding out whether
the Tsangpo flowed into the Brahmaputra. To that end,
the pundit and a companion whose name appeared in the
archives under the initials N.S. were to penetrate the wilder
reaches of the Himalayas disguised as pilgrims, and launch
into the Tsangpo five hundred marked logs of wood, at the
rate of fifty a day, over a ten-day period. Meanwhile, an
observer posted on the Brahmaputra would be waiting for
the logs' appearance to confirm the confluence of the two
rivers.

Given the almost Buddhist simplicity of that descrip-
tion, the mission of Kintup and his companion had no

reason to fail. But it was the early stages of the expedition that ran into all-too-familiar complications which the Great Trigonometrical Survey would like to forget. In those days, entering Nepal was as perilous as infiltrating the trenches of a cruel and suspicious enemy. Various gurus had tried it in the past, only to pay with their lives for a sparse return of measurements and discoveries of little significance. Added to the secrecy of the Tibetans and the zeal of the Russians to win the race to map Nepal through espionage and all kinds of deceptions were the precarious conditions awaiting those travelers who, to top it all, had to be astute enough to conceal delicate and cumbersome surveying instruments in their false monks' robes. In a word, Kintup's mission was close to suicidal, yet he had embarked on it with a willingness bordering on monomania.

When I realized that the archives of the Royal Geographical Society would throw no further light on Kintup's mission, I devoted my time to looking for some new account, some clear indication of its circumstances and its consequences. Needless to say, the majority of my superiors knew nothing of the details of that distant expedition, not even of the pundit's existence. It is true that one of them seemed to remember his name from the accounts of those who first discovered certain primitive paths of access to Tibet from the west, but soon enough Kintup and his exploits began to seem no more than a product of the inflamed imagination of Colonel Bailey. If that were not enough, when at last I had the opportunity to ask

Younghusband himself, who was then president of the Royal Geographical Society, about the person who had discovered the confluence of the two rivers, Tsangpo and Brahmaputra, he replied without hesitation that that discovery came about through the heroic labors of an expedition led in 1868 by Captain Thomas G. Montgomerie.

Where then did that leave the pundit Kintup and his anonymous traveling companion? Who was the tailor of Darjeeling who had refused the thousand rupees from my chief? The only certain way of knowing the truth, I realized, was to return to Nepal to confront Kintup himself. I have to say that at this point nothing appealed to me less than returning to carry on the work of my late chief. In some way or other, the specters of Bailey and Kintup had driven me to the conviction that there was no effort in life that was really worth making. Now my whole existence had turned into a meaningless journey in which glory, recognition on the part of my peers, and the advancement of the mapping of Tibet to counteract the imminent advance of the Russians were much less important to me than the single intent to understand the sacrifice of a man whom no one remembered or would ever remember. But unfortunately that man was to be found in British India, and it was for that reason alone that I finally bowed to the wishes of my superiors and embarked once again on my journey south.

I arrived in Nepal in the early days of December, only to find that the old tailor had died a little after my visit to him. The young Nepalese who had fallen heir to his workshop in Darjeeling was unable to tell me the circumstances of his predecessor's death, but it was not difficult to imagine his agonies in the gloom of the tailor's shop, his dead body wearing that same smile, half indifferent, half mocking, with which he had sent me away months before. Once again, I had that feeling of being utterly alone, having reached a block it would be difficult to get beyond. There was only one lead to follow before I surrendered to total despair, but it seemed so remote that it was some days before I gave it my whole attention: one morning, while I was preparing my return to Bombay, I was trying to imagine for a last time Kintup's Himalayan journey, and it was then that I lit on the figure at his side, his companion in misfortune who, perhaps through being unnamed in the archives, had slipped to the edge of my memory. Surprised at my carelessness, like a sailor adrift in a storm, I dwelt at length on the possibility that the man might have outlived Kintup. Even so, the whole enterprise seemed as ambitious as the journey Kintup himself took, but I realized that at this stage that was precisely what drew me to it. So, feeling like someone on the verge of diving into a vast black hole, I set about tracking the whereabouts of Kintup's companion, even if it were to take my whole life.

While I was searching for the second pundit, with more effort than success, the Royal Geographical Society began to be concerned over my slowness in taking up Colonel Bailey's cartographic labors. Once more the Russians had managed to get hold of confidential information on the most recent British incursions into the territory, and it was now rumored that before long the forces of the Czar would invade Tibet to put an end to a geographical race that had already gone on too long. I think I have already made clear how little I was concerned at that time over my military and map-making duties in Nepal. While it is true that in the past such an obligation would have seemed to me an imperative in my pursuit of glory, now the only thing that interested me was to learn the particulars of Kintup's journey, just as Bailey had been obsessed with finding out the details of my visit to Darjeeling. All in all, the difference between the fixation of my old chief and the one that possessed me was that I, to put a rest to my anxieties, had first to find a nameless pundit in a far corner of the world.

In Darjeeling, Kintup's neighbors had appeared reluctant at first to give me any information about the second pundit, and what they finally told me, with the encouragement of a bribe, was sparse indeed. From them I found out that the said N.S. was a cousin of Kintup's, and that after giving up his cartographic endeavours, he had left years earlier for Bombay. I was overcome with joy at the hope of finding, with some luck, the missing man still alive, although the funds which the Royal Geographical Society had advanced me to further my explorations had dwindled in an alarming manner and I was afraid I would still have to cross a number of palms to find the man I sought. I confess that more than once I was tempted to dip into the thousand rupees that Kintup would not accept and that Bailey had never bothered to ask for; but so obsessed was I with the notion of handing them over intact to the pundit's cousin that I even went hungry during the time I still had to spend in India looking for the man.

Bombay would certainly have been my last port of call on the way to despair had it not been for the providential intervention of the head porter at the Great Trigonometrical Survey. The old man must have felt some sympathy for my efforts and disappointments, for one afternoon he made the discreet suggestion to me that before I left I should ask about N.S. among the old pundits who on their return from Nepal had found work on the payroll of the Russian embassy in India. It was no secret that a substantial number of local explorers, originally under contract to the Russians, had for some time been infiltrating the ranks of the Great Trigonometrical Survey with the sole purpose of undermining the progress of the British and getting hold of the information they had gathered through the efforts of their pundits. It was difficult for me to believe that Kintup or his companion could have had anything to do with Russian counterintelligence, but things were such that I could not turn my back on any possibility, and that was the last one I had left.

Luckily for me, or perhaps unluckily, the porter had been right on target. After some days spent overcoming resistance with my dwindling funds, I established the fact that a pundit by the name of Nain Singh had played an important part in exploring the Tsangpo, and on his return had worked for the Russians for several years. Not only was he still alive; he also enjoyed a quite comfortable old age in a Bombay suburb, where he had retired to enjoy a pension that was well worthy of his employers.

The first thought I had on at last coming across Nain Singh was that his relative well-being seemed quite disgusting compared to the memories I still saved of my journey to Darjeeling. Plump and talkative, Kintup's cousin gave me the impression from the very beginning that he had attained his success in the most questionable manner and, worse, was unabashedly proud of the fact. As soon as I explained to him the reason for my visit, he acknowledged that he had been a part of Kintup's odyssey, but he warned me right away that he was not permitted to go into any detail about the excursion, which, even now, had to be regarded as a military secret. I listened to his warning, trying not to worry; then I shrugged my shoulders and told him that while I regretted his excessive concern, I had made the long journey from London for the precise purpose of bringing to him a thousand rupees, with the condition that he help to clear up certain aspects of that mission to the Himalayas which, I argued, had no importance any longer beyond the merely historical.

I must not have concealed my anxiety too well, for after he had heard me, Nain Singh hesitated barely a second before bursting out in a hoot of laughter such as can come only from cynics and murderers. He immediately expressed, with a certain irony, his gratification at the Royal Geographical Society's concern for the well-being of its poor pundits, but he added that, before he talked, I had to swear by all that is sacred that I would hand over the thousand rupees regardless of how much he could tell me about his years with Kintup. Once that was agreed, the old pundit settled himself in a vast leather armchair and told me directly what I longed to hear.

With Kintup, he began, he had been recruited more than thirty years ago by the Great Trigonometrial Survey, which, after a thorough training, had in fact sent them to Nepal to find out if the Tsangpo flowed into the Brahmaputra. Disguised as Tibetan lamas, they entered the territory of the Himalayas, but not long after the journey came to an abrupt halt when he, Nain Singh, sold his cousin as a slave to a horse dealer, who paid thirty rupees for him.

If the fat pundit expected some recrimination from me when he reached that part of his story, that is something that matters little in my story. Rather than penitent, Nain Singh seemed well satisfied with what he had done, so much so that the further adventurings of his cousin seemed quite stupid to him. He seemed somewhat put out when he told me that Kintup had not allowed himself to be outwitted by the betrayal, but instead, some months later, managed to escape from his master and set out again, only to be recaptured in the vicinity of the Marpung monastery. Taking pity on his misfortune, a lama agreed to buy him for fifty rupees, on condition that Kintup work for him to pay off the debt. Which the hardworking pundit did for several months, until one day he asked the lama's permission to go on a pilgrimage. Impressed by his devotion, the lama gave him leave, and Kintup then made straight for the Tsangpo, on the banks of which he prepared the five hundred marked logs he was to throw in the river. Regrettably, the spot picked out as an observer's post on the Brahmaputra had not been available for some time, so that Kintup hid the marked logs in a cave and returned to the monastery to wait for a chance to send a messenger to Darjeeling to inform the members of the Great Trigonometrical Survey. Months later, the pundit once more sought the lama's permission to set out on another pilgrimage, although this time he made for Lhasa in search of a friend, a merchant by whom he might send a letter to his superiors announcing his plan to launch the logs from Bipung between the fifth and fifteenth day of the tenth Tibetan month. In Lhasa, however, Kintup received firm news that Montgomerie's expedition had finally proved, through another approach, the confluence of the Tsangpo and the Brahmaputra, as well as word that his mother had died, believing him to have been lost in carrying out his mission.

Nain Singh had no inclination to speculate on what passed through his cousin's head in that moment. Four years had gone by since his departure, his body by now carried the indelible traces that the Himalayas exact, and his spirit wavered now between the sustenance of prayer and the mortifications of betrayal or pain. If he made the decision at that point to send the letter and carry out what he had promised, he did it certainly as much out of pride as out of despair. It would be difficult for the poor man to go on exploring that territory, but nobody would be able to say of him that he had failed in his mission. So it was that, on the appointed dates, the exhausted pundit returned to the Tsangpo and cast into the river the five hundred marked logs that floated away on the current, with no one stationed any longer on the Brahmaputra to watch them eventually pass.

At that point in his story, Nain Singh revealed a momentary flash of deep respect for the memory of his cousin that almost immediately gave way to his mocking smile. As for me, I had to confess to the same admiration Colonel Bailey had felt in the past. At last, I began to understand my old chief's firm belief that true heroism shows itself spontaneously somewhere in the space between courage and absurdity. Strange as it may seem, Kintup's attitude in the Himalayas made perfect sense to me. What did not fit at all in the whole story was Kintup's later refusal to accept the colonel's thousand rupees and Nain Singh's betrayal of his cousin for a sum of money that even for him was quite paltry.

Toward the end of the conversation, both questions were answered in the most terrible way. No sooner had I handed over to Nain Singh the money I had promised him than he ceremoniously removed thirty rupees and returned them to me with the request that they should be turned over to Colonel Bailey sahib. Surprised at hearing my chief's name from the lips of that man, and realizing with some horror the message implied in that gesture, I replied that the colonel had died some months before. This time it was Nain Singh who showed a deep interest in hearing the details of the death of Bailey, with whom he assured me he had a very close connection at the time of the Tsangpo expedition. Then he asked me point-blank if Bailey had been buried in Russia, at which I, somewhat wary of understanding what was behind that question, replied indignantly that the colonel had been buried in London with full honors. At that, the fat little pundit broke into a smile and snatched back from me the thirty rupees he had offered me. Then he puffed out his cheeks, gave a long whistle, and exclaimed with undisguised admiration that that Bailey, that goddamned Bailey, was the biggest son of a bitch in all creation.

Hagiography of the Apostate

Frequently, Brother Jean Degard would wake at sunset out of a long dream, and the fading light of the Libyan desert would enter him till he felt that some heavenly spirit, pitying his crime and his sufferings, was enveloping him in a lost and wavering clarity of mind. At the fall of night, however, objects took back their proper proportions in the gloom of the cave, reminding the hermit that he had not turned his back on his century to reach for divine light but to confront the darkness at its most dire. In these moments, the embrace of an angel or the worship of a burning bush, proffering a forgiveness of which he knew himself to be unworthy, would have been of little use to him. What he needed to do was tempt the devil himself, summoning up the dark spirit in all his wretched meanness.

The day of his departure, the Abbot Gauthier had sought him out in his cell to urge him not to leave the monastery of La Clochette, assuring him that nobody had ever set eyes on the devil in that wilderness where a man would be sharing his solitude with grasshoppers and crows, and only if he managed to survive the scimitars of the Tuaregs. But the warning went unheeded in the mind of the would-be hermit. Convinced that his rotting soul would one way or other attract evil spirits, Brother Degard reminded the abbot that his hands were already stained with blood, so that the pardon of God or of men counted for little with him. What he was seeking was oblivion, and oblivion, he added, was something he could attain, not with the force that God had denied him when he was most in need, but by attempting the utter surrender of his will. And he ended by saying, as he made a bundle out of his few belongings, that out there, where they could put up with a murderer, there had to be a devil.

Once installed in his cave, Degard settled down to wait for the devils to appear. Months passed unnoticed, days and nights of fasting in which the ascetic began to fear that the devil might have in fact forgotten that state in which someone will summon him without being suffi-ciently sinful to deserve him. Degard sensed the passing of the hours as his eyes wandered over the landscape, calling on the devil by each of his known names, or by others that he himself had invented from a mishmash of Latin and Arabic, tracing arcane circles in the sand and burning in-cense until he had used up his store of matches. His pale Breton peasant's skin took on a deep tan from his exposure to the open air, waiting for the peckings of nonexistent succubi, and his worm-eaten spirit broke out on his skin in the form of blisters that gushed blood, a liquid discharge that he in his madness took to be only a physical mani-festation of the unsheddable memory of his crime. Meanwhile, the desert remained impervious, and Degard decided then that the devil's most fiendish twist lay in his utter indifference toward those who cried out to him. Not to be present to anyone or for anyone, not even to relish a perdition long anticipated. That was what most vexed the hermit; and that was why he went on abasing himself just as fiercely as he cursed the devil's absence.

On a certain night Degard mistook the torches of a caravan for the manifestation of a spirit from another world, come in search of him, and he left the cave in a gesture of welcome. His appearance, his cries, his drooling and cursing had the opposite effect on the Tuaregs, for, taking him for a devil, they fled the place, invoking the protection of their god. It was then that Degard, once more immersed in his solitude, saw that the indifference of the desert should be understood rather as a message in code, an invitation to him to find in the stretches of his devastated spirit the ingredients necessary to create the devil. From his sins, from his sins alone, a monstrous creature would have to emerge, formed from pieces of his live flesh blended with a steady flow of remorse. In short, he would be the father and creator of evil, for only so could he confront the devil and recognize himself in that face.

At first the hermit imagined that bringing the devil into being would be fairly easy, but in fact his invocation alone took much more time and effort than he had expected. To summon the Dark One was no longer a matter of plural names and charts of the stars. He had to give himself up to remembering his own wrongdoings, to that excremental stench that Degard at times confused with the disquieting odor of sanctity. Perhaps in this way, with a measure of patience, he would rescue himself from his own affliction and cause its darkness to lift from his spirit.

Finally, one day, the hermit's fits stopped being mystical experiences and turned into epilepsy. The devil then frothed at the lips and settled himself expectantly in the depths of the cave. His creator spent hours gazing at him, wondering why his guest remained as still as a statue. Mean and hunchbacked, wrapped in a djellaba that to Degard looked altogether too like the one his onetime victim had worn, the devil did no more than return his gaze, all the time gnawing on a goldfinch wing. His replies to the hermit were so laconic that it was not even possible to make out which language he was speaking, and Degard was at his wits' end looking for a way to startle his creature out of its apathy.

One afternoon, almost at the point of giving up and asking for pardon, Degard decided that the only way to challenge his devil was in the persona of a saint. Where before he had invoked evil, now he had to conjure up a saint to rouse the anger of the other and allow himself to tangle with him on the sand floor muddied by their own urine.

Creating a saint was for Degard much more arduous than his previous task—his invocation of the devil had almost drained him of the remains of his virtue. So he had to relive the times of his childhood, and from there progress in his memory to the monastery of La Clochette.

Thus, slowly and in pain, he brought it about that one day the devil stopped gnawing on his goldfinch wing and inclined his head toward a reawakened man whose sanctity had finally summoned him out of his lethargy.

With the creation of the saint, things changed dramatically. Before any physical confrontation, there first arose a more devastating intellectual one between the two of them. Materializing in the cave, the saint decided to confront the devil using his own logic, and drive him to a combat in which Degard's spirit would devour itself. He began one night by posing questions to the devil that at first seemed inoffensive and somewhat byzantine, which the devil answered sometimes with simple tricks of language, sometimes with tedious sophisms. Satisfied that he had understood the rules of the game, the saint then began to complicate the questions with the pleasure a chess player takes in playing a game against himself, trying to play fair and to cheat at the same time for the game to count. Very soon the rules and the trials of the game had so clarified themselves that saint and devil both worked out in the end a tacit agreement that each had to observe for their mutual convenience. From a position of moral objectivity, the hermit first formulated a theological question that he, playing the saint, would try to answer with the help of a truth; and then, immediately assuming the role of devil, he would go about destroying that truth with arguments convincing enough to undermine the original logic of the saint.

The nature of evil, the existence of God and his connections to nothingness, the impotence of a Being omnipotent enough to create a rock so huge that its creator could not lift it, predestination, and, above all, the inequity between blame and pardon were only some of the dilemmas that came up in the interminable game of Brother Jean Degard. Sometimes the very nature of the questions caused saint and devil to spend entire weeks without reaching agreement, for the contest was logically balanced, and the truths rationally achieved by the saint could always be countered when the devil's arguments were up to it. They were drawn more always to the theological debates, and if on some occasion the devil tried to pull a trick, introducing in mid-debate a carnal temptation or a reminder of Degard's crime, the game came to a halt, and both players ended up exchanging apologies in order to resume what now took up their entire existences.

With the passing of the months, Brother Degard managed to dissolve all memory of his crime in the ins and outs of the combat. His life and the bloodiest details from his past suddenly moved to the territory of forgetting, where they might well have vanished had not Degard at that moment come up with a question he would later regret. The hermit himself could never understand what drove him to do it, but it is quite possible that it may have indicated a certain wish to put an end to a game that in the end he knew could not last forever. Perhaps that night, betrayed by memory, Degard might have recognized in the face of the devil the features of the man he had murdered, and thought that getting rid of him would succeed in removing the last obstacle to his happiness. However it was, this time the hermit had the saint tempt the devil by questioning the very existence of evil. The debate went on until dawn. Devil and saint used their best arguments, they raged and they reasoned, until Degard came up with a professed belief that claimed the devil did not exist and that consequently there was no hell to punish his crime or wash the blood from his hands. As for the devil, when he had heard the saint's arguments, he realized the threat that was hanging over the game, and from his love of permanence he presented with a near-divine clarity arguments that proved that it was the saint, not he, who did not exist.

Brother Degard never did get to know the results of the contest, for both attempts at proof led him inevitably to conclude that neither the devil nor the saint could ever exist, could ever have existed. Hence, the Abbot Gauthier could insist on declaring, among other things, that nobody had ever seen the devil in that wasteland where a hermit could expect to share his solitude only with grasshoppers and crows.

A Bestiary

They would arrive, delighted and somewhat dazed, from Inverness, Manchester, and London, disembarking at Cape Town, and immediately making for the mine in the Kalahari. So eager were they to find the cavern that they would probably have descended on their own, had not the authorities taken the precaution to surround it with wire fencing and eagle-eyed lookouts. One by one they would bring their fuming vehicles to a stop, move closer, and read with alien eyes an order in which Their Majesties forbade the taking of photographs in the depths of the mine, for fear that tungsten light might cause irreparable damage to the creatures which for years or perhaps for centuries had multiplied peaceably there in the darkness and the cold. A string of red lights some meters above the opening was enough to give visitors a glimpse of the depths of the cavern, fully warned as they always were that any inadvertency would be punished, inasmuch as it endangered the creatures and those who were studying them.

But not even a promise to obey the rules to the letter could guarantee that visitors gained entrance to the mine.

Many of the curious returned home without having descended to the abyss that had opened in the wounded belly of the Kalahari; and there was even some lawyer from Chelsea who in this vein denounced the withholding of visiting privileges by the authorities as colonial self-importance. As for the few chosen ones who did receive permission to descend into the mine, they had to submit to innumerable levels of control that some of them considered a humiliation. These men and women, used to having their way with a mere inflection of the voice, had to complete in silence extensive questionnaires, sign contracts worthy of a state of siege, display safe-conducts with many-headed stamps, and leave as security landholdings they had saved for a dignified and unruffled old age. Similarly, their breasts had to suffer the cold touch of metal stethoscopes, and their bodies, never before exposed to the weather, had to be washed down with turpentine before they donned the rough wool cloaks they would wear for the descent.

Even so, not even these payments and tortures could ever guarantee that these temporary Franciscans would ever come face-to-face with the creatures. There were many visitors who returned to the surface with no more to console them than having heard out of the darkness a brief laugh or the echo of a spine-chilling groan from some niche in the rock. Out of breath, and disinclined to admit failure, it was those very travelers who chose to feed the appetites of the press with a real bestiary of unearthly beings woven from the fears of their infancy—weird, reptilian forms, hybrids of wolves and bats, unlikely mosaics of disconnected claws, fur, and fangs that had gleamed before their eyes in the reddish light from the upper level. One aged visitor chose to describe, with the enthusiasm of a mythomaniac, open jaws that gave off the unbearable stench of death, eyes like burning coals, and a scaly skin that had scraped the cheeks of a hysterical adolescent who in reality had fainted on entering the mine.

Certainly, it was the frenzy and the overflowing imagination of those who felt cheated that kept the press from paying much attention to those who had seen something, those singled out by misfortune who ascended again to the light of the Kalahari to regret their boldness for the remainder of their lives. With the cold and the stench of rot from below, these unfortunate souls were forced to add to their memories a terrifying vision that went much further in than their eyes and took deep root in their being. None of them had been able to glimpse the creatures for more than the second it took for them to sigh or to sneeze, but that moment was enough for the group to return to the surface like those coming up from the deep sea for air. Meanwhile, the beasts shifted in their nests, scratched at the mud with nervous claws, and hid themselves in a panic, sobbing and groaning like children in the grip of some dreadful pain.

They say that there was an occasion when the visitors were able to come face-to-face with one of the creatures, which they later realized was blind. It flew considerably higher than was usual, so much so that it was unable to resist the enthusiastic applause of the visitors watching its clumsy fluttering against the wall of the cavern. Driven mad by the noise and by desperation, the creature perished in midair, after spreading its wings and showing its visage to a gathering that immediately closed its eyes in an attempt to wipe out what showed in those features. It was neither the stench nor the pelt nor the fangs, nor the creature's animal nature, that struck them with such fear. It was an all-too-human transparency about the face that imprinted itself on their minds, hoping desperately as they ascended that the elevator could bear the added heaviness of their spirits. A press photograph taken of that group immediately after shows a woman vomiting blood in front of a dozen grinning bushmen. If you look closely at that same photograph, in the distance you can make out the silhouettes of two men who that afternoon went in search of a tree stout enough to support the weight of their bodies, under the impassive brilliance of the Southern Cross.

Amends in Halak-Proot

In August of that same year, E. A. Talbot, a graduate in medicine from the University of Cardiff, boarded the ship *Seagull* with the firm intention of never again setting foot on European soil. Scarcely three weeks had passed since he had failed for the second time to pass his examination for an appointment as surgeon in the British Army, which left him in the humiliating situation of watching his father's regiment embark without him, bound for the Afghanistan front, where it was predicted that General Talbot and his riflemen would win a glorious triumph at very little cost to them. It may be true that the young doctor, the coast of England already behind him, had no particular inkling at that moment of just how many casualties Afghan lances would cause the British Army, but this bloody circumstance would not in fact have altered his resolve to turn his back on Europe forever. Not even his father's defeat had been able to erase from his brow the scar of shame that he hoped to bury deep in the jungles of Java, where the Dutch government, less particular in their judgments than their British counterparts when it came to hiring, had just appointed him as administrator of a psychiatric hospital. It bothered him little that his colleagues spoke of that posting as something like a prison sentence, but young Talbot, used to scorn from childhood on, secretly nursed the hope that the patients in Halak-Proot would prove more civilized in their behavior than his compatriots. It was true that a certain aura of suicide hung over the appointment, but Talbot at least had the consolation of knowing that, for his family, distance would dim the memory of his mediocrity.

The new administrator disembarked in Surabaya in mid-October, and immediately traveled inland, mainly to discover the gap between his expectations and the reality. More than a hospital, the psychiatric establishment of Halak-Proot was an old factory building with five long hallways that the Dutch colonists, for want of a more appropriate or perhaps a more sordid place, had reconditioned badly, to house some hundred officers who had lost their wits on diverse allied fronts from Indochina to Micronesia. Although among the patients were some colonists less lost in their eccentricities than others, the truth is that all traces of civilization and the civilized dissolved into a blurred mass of stammering ghosts who did nothing but pace the long hallways, taking turns. Watching them, Talbot could not suppress a shudder, although for the first time he had the feeling that his arrival in the hell of the insane could not be simply a matter of chance. In one of the *Seagull*'s ports of call, Talbot had received some news of the casualties the Afghan front had inflicted on the British troops, but even so he was sure that his father would soon return to London in triumph, as if to under-score the humiliation of a son usually caught up in absurd enterprises, who, to cap it all, was now fading away in the Antipodes in a confused company of lunatics, who were incapable even of controlling themselves. No question of it, thought Talbot as he contemplated the wandering pa-tients of Halak-Proot, this must be the last and the worst of all possible worlds, and it was precisely here and for that reason that he would come across his chance to face up triumphantly to a destiny that until then had been adver-sarial.

The first report that the incensed administrator sent to his Dutch superiors already shows an eagerness only to be expected in saints or the dying. On carefully numbered pages, in a handwriting much too careful for an English doctor, the young man expounded to his superiors on mat-ters that they certainly knew well enough. The Halak-Proot Hospital, Talbot began by saying, had gone through numerous modifications from its beginnings, but he added that these changes were barely noticeable or merely sym-bolic at best. Every three or four years, a new adminis-trator arrived with an escort of assistants either drunk or brutish, the majority of them old-time Irish convicts mar-ried to prostitutes from Guinea, thugs with bad skin and worse habits, who never differed very much from their predecessors. It could well happen that a new administra-tor would come across a pair of warders or a morphine-addicted doctor with some faint influence in political circles, but on most occasions the members of the previous

administration had to flee the island to avoid being themselves imprisoned in the galleries where their onetime victims would beat out of them whatever sense they had left.

In a like way, the hospital's physical plant was customarily subjected to fanciful remodelings: the walls repainted
yellow, the emergency rooms and operating rooms given a
tidying, a dozen Aborigines repairing the straitjackets with
twine, and the cooks conscientiously studying the possibil-
ities of an even more repellent menu than the previous
one, no matter the cost. In such circumstances, Talbot's report went on, it was understandable that the groans, the
hallucinations, and the sufferings of the patients at Halak-
Proot might stay as they were, or even worse. Brought
back from wars always longer and bloodier, the veterans
took their turns day after day along the galleries, and their
madness settled on them with the same success with
which the remodelings had settled on the jungle, by making its existence more ominous. Neither corporal pun-
ishment nor the attention of concerned doctors could
therefore solve the problem of overcrowding that plagued
the hospital: after lengthy examination, the diagnosis was
almost always positive, even in the case of those suspected
of faking a psychosis, preferring to be interned over going
to war. It could be said, all in all, that Halak-Proot func-
tioned as a kind of underworld whose oblivion attracted
and nourished all the madness in the southwest, for its
very existence seemed to be enough to let loose the germ
of insanity in those who fought at the front under the constant threat of ending their days in a place where even

those in charge could behave only as though mentally disturbed.

Dr. Talbot was not overly upset that this and his other reports received no reply beyond a curt acknowledgment of receipt, written in Dutch. He knew he had not drafted those interminable reports with any hope of changing the attitudes of those above him, but more to put his own ideas in order and leave a record of the whole situation which he now had to confront. So these reports were followed by many others in which the young doctor, aware of his own inadequacies, set himself to deal with every one of the cases that swamped his hospital, until he ended by analyzing his own oddnesses in nights thick with mosquitoes, punctured by howls that came either from the galleries or from his own throat, he could not tell.

It is not in the least fanciful to think that young Talbot might have in fact fallen into a state of madness even deeper than that of his patients, had his destiny not then taken a spectacular turn. Half a year after Talbot's arrival in Java, the captain of the *Seagull* brought him a telegram in which his mother told him that General Ernest Talbot had died of dysentery in London. Most unexpectedly, the old man had left to him his country house on the fringes of Wales, for which reason his family urged him to return to England at once to occupy his new estate. Talbot, however, remained firm in his promise never to return to Europe. He sent off his instructions to the executors, and as soon as the money from the sale was at his disposition, he set to work with a new passion that little resembled that with which he had drafted his reports on how things stood in Halak-Proot.

It seems that from then on the Dutch heard no more firm news from Halak-Proot. They never again received a single line in the handwriting of the administrator, whose venturings they learned of only months later, when some wood merchants surprised them with the news that the hospital had changed radically. The whole region talked about how the English administrator of Halak-Proot had used every last cent of his fortune to transform the hospital into a private paradise: the padded cells and the trepanning rooms had been totally demolished, and in their place Dr. Talbot had created dreamlike gardens with lawns of the finest English grass, pinewood walks, and pools of warm water where exquisitely beautiful girls and young men brought from Hong Kong waited to please the patients. Where before the five inhospitable halls had stood, now there were Turkish baths with accommodating masseuses, a small hippodrome, and a casino with liveried attendants, with whom Talbot had replaced the guards. It was also reported that even the administrator of the hospital had acquired the air of a gentleman: he had grown not just a beard but bushy side-whiskers, where his first white hairs gave him a noble aspect. His hospital gown had yielded to Italian suits; and even the frames of his glasses gleamed in the jungle like a pair of Spanish doubloons in the dark of the deep ocean.

Hearing this story, Talbot's Dutch superiors decided that he had finally lost his mind, and they predicted the total and utter collapse of his attempts to improve the lot of the patients. But before two months had passed, they realized the doctor in Surabaya was no amateur, and that his reforms of the hospital were not aimed at redeeming his patients so much as driving them away with alacrity from Halak-Proot. No sooner had the image of this new European paradise in the midst of an oceanic inferno spread throughout the region than the cases of dementia began to decrease surprisingly; and if indeed some people believed that this miracle was due to the humane treatment that Dr. Talbot's hospital now provided, it was soon clear that the real treatment lay in not accepting anyone there who was not clearly and irredeemably insane. Suddenly soldiers and officers in the southwest began to take note of their own mental irregularities, some twist of mind that might someday open the doors of Halak-Proot to them; and it was precisely that fiction, that desperate search for a passport to paradise, that led them to exercise and build up a most exasperating sanity. More and more, the new doctors Talbot brought to his hospital discovered that the cases of dementia they examined were mere stage acts, blatant deceptions on the part of those whose only recourse was to accept the inevitable, their sentence to sanity.

So it was by that chance that Dr. Talbot's hospital came to be a kind of closed paradise, as closed as hell or, certainly, as the spirit of the person who conceived it. In that tantalizing reflection of his Antipodes, there was room only for a custodian and a guard who, bursting with resentment, grew old there, strolling every morning among exceptional birches and smiling beatifically at those who managed to look over the walls. Talbot, they say, would scan these intrusive faces a moment and study them until they dissolved into the twilight of a cambano tree that would never again blemish his English garden. Then the old doctor would smile to himself and watch night fall, as he circled the paths lined by elms that had grown where the long halls of Halak-Proot had once stood.

About Our Flour

His Excellency the Ambassador has every justification when he declares our flour to be the tastiest in the whole Empire, and I can assure all of you that any one of us would not hesitate to do battle with those who dared to say otherwise. The blessings of our flour, my friends, are merely a reflection of the virtues of our people, a divine reward for the humanity we showed in relieving the extreme hunger that for five years plagued our lands, lands abandoned by God and Their Majesties. And if what I say seems to be singing our own praises, I ask you to remember in our favor that even the Erlings, those creatures as ill-favored in appearance as they are rich in understanding, publicly acknowledged our benevolence when we answered their need in those lean and miserable times.

Of course, my friends, I am well aware that no community is perfect, and ours is no exception. Any city, however reserved, can count in its archives painful happenings, like the one which has brought together this distinguished gathering. I can however assure you that the death of our lieutenant was no fault of any one of us, but rather the sad consequence of these ill-fated times. We his neighbors did everything possible to save him, but there are times when madness rapidly takes over, treacherously and in secret. How were we to know that this man's judgment was failing, when the minds of all of us here were weakened by the hunger that had spread east of the Indian Ocean? In those days, the furious gales from Anangaypur were blowing alarmingly close to us. There were uprisings from Cairo to Sri Lanka. Hunger had weakened us to a point where we seemed a nation of ghosts. Every morning we had to line up in the market for hours to get our rations of filthy water and bread so hard that not even the rats would gnaw it. From the continent we received only letters in which our chancellor urged us to put up with these painful trials for as long as the Empire honored its promise to fund the campaign in the Caucasus. In truth, my friends, nobody then had time to worry over a poor soul like the lieutenant, who patrolled our streets clutching a black leather suitcase and talking to it as if it were a baby at the breast. I won't deny that such behavior in itself is odd and dangerous, but the times seemed even more so. A few months earlier, the Erlings had come down from the foothills begging for shelter, although many in the city could not understand why the authorities had decided to open our doors to such repugnant creatures, who, it was said, would soon finish off the little food we had left. Those fears prompted the governor to explain to us that, besides paying a residence tax, the Erlings would feed only on our leavings, a condition that the majority of us accepted, even applauding the opportunity to show the whole Empire that our city, though remote, was a civilized place. Even so, there were some who refused to recognize the even-handedness of our treatment of the Erlings, and of these, unquestionably, our lieutenant was a prime example.

At the urgent request of the ambassador, we have reopened the lieutenant's dossier, and now we can state with certainty that it is the account of an admirable young man, a worthy member of the Second Infantry Battalion, which brought glory to us all in Ceylon. Perhaps life had been a bit hard on him, especially where women were concerned, although that would not keep us from acknowledging him as one of us. It was his record, gentlemen, and not just chance, that caused his superiors to make the well-meaning mistake of appointing him Chief of Customs in our city precisely when the Erlings were arriving. Consider if you will the thousands of safe-conducts and other legal documents that this veteran of fierce fighting suddenly had to confront, God knows how, with no one to translate for him the incomprehensible language of these strange guests, burdened with offspring even uglier than themselves. It seems to me, gentlemen, that a few hours of work like that would drive the sanest man mad, more so our lieutenant, from whom life demanded many sacrifices without bringing him much gratification. I don't know if he had a chance to be informed of the sanitary advantages the Erlings were offering us, but unquestionably his fevered mind set up its defenses against this sudden flood of other beings, who looked not just strange but even hostile. Perhaps, when his frantic workdays ended, he went back to his miserable room in the port, threw himself on his bunk, and gave himself up to a wild conjecturing, in which causes and effects never fitted. He dreamed at times that the Erlings dirtied everything they touched, that they bred with the characteristic frenzy of lesser beings, that they were eating away at the little food and peace of mind that were left to him. One worthy woman insisted it was just after the Erlings had arrived when she first saw the lieutenant wandering the streets clutching his wretched suitcase, cursing and gasping as if the Erlings were stealing the last few blocks of air the city was saving for him. He let his beard grow, his boots go unpolished, and his official coat turn into a shapeless rag, its colors dissolved by tears, saliva, and sweat. In brief, the man went completely mad in just a few days, and it was obvious that what had set off his madness was nothing other than the presence of the Erlings in our city.

A few weeks later came winter, and with it the wind from Anangaypur in all its fury. As our hunger grew, so did the loose suspicion, not just in the lieutenant but in many citizens, that the Erlings were to blame for our ills. All at once people began to charge the Erlings with terrible crimes committed at night while, in plain daylight, these guests of ours behaved so politely as to seem suspicious to some. Once more it was necessary for the governor to make clear that the Erlings were not here to harm us, but that first they deserved credit for keeping the city so clean of our leavings, and for gaining us a reputation for mercy.

Unfortunately, the lieutenant could not hear these recent explanations, for by then he had cut himself off from the world, in his small cell by the port. It was not long before his neighbors, decent, honest people, were pressing their ears to the wall and listening to the scandalous love talk he addressed to the treasure in his suitcase. Don't worry, he was saying, I'll look out for you, I'll nurse you into life, and I'll fly with you beyond these miserable walls, where nobody can harm us. Then, they said, the man burst into tears, and there was no way of shutting him up until morning.

That's where things stood when fortune chose to play the lieutenant his last bad card. Bit by bit, the Erlings had set themselves up in the cemetery, and truth to tell, they made a good job of cleaning up all our trash. They were very well behaved, and they even began to grasp our language, awkward words, but enough for them to keep pressing their thanks on us. But some of our neighbors were wary. There was something offensive about these effusions, which they chose to interpret not as gratitude but as veiled mockery. There was no reason for it, but you know how people behave in times of crisis. They become suspicious; and if they don't find a reason here for what's wrong, they'll find it there. I tell you this, gentlemen, so you will understand when the lieutenant's neighbors finally lost their patience and denounced him, their lives disturbed by his weeping and his constant accusations that they, the others, were after his precious suitcase. So urgent were the complaints of these poor men and women about the lieutenant's madness that the authorities could do nothing more than send around officers to put an end to the whole troubling affair.

But fate had other things in mind, and that very afternoon a bunch of hot-headed citizens suddenly turned for no particular reason on a family of Erlings who had the bad luck to be passing at that moment in front of the lines of people waiting for rations in the market. In immediate response, a large group of Erlings made for the plaza to seek justice for their dead, but chaos had taken hold of the city in such a way that the disturbance got out of hand. Nobody, my friends, will ever know if the Erlings were in fact armed. These were not the times for questions, let alone for allowing anyone to destroy the peace of the city with impunity. If the governor did order his guard to fire on the Erlings, remember in his defense that the Erlings could not after all be considered human, and it could not even be said, as some slanderers do, that blood was shed, for the Erlings, as you well know, leave behind when they die only that white flour, which that day covered the plaza from top to bottom, and which today is so pleasing to the palate.

I need take up no more of your attention with details of which, dear friends, you are fully aware. What matters here is that, on that very afternoon, the lieutenant, terrified by the shouting and the commotion the Erlings were causing in the streets, left his retreat and climbed the highest bell tower of the cathedral, still clutching his suit-case. The police followed, climbing the bell tower after him at the risk of their lives; and when they tried to seize his treasure, the demented lieutenant threw himself from the tower. He was rushed to hospital, but died minutes later, shouting for his suitcase and muttering that they, the others, had taken it, unaware that finally we had found the remedy for all our distress. Needless to say, gentle-men, the poor devil's suitcase contained nothing but a huge stork's egg that had shattered in the unlucky lieu-tenant's fall, leaving on the air of our beautiful city only the aftersmell of reeking tar and ruin.

The Chinaman with the Heads

E ven now, when I bring him to mind and remember precisely every one of his gestures or his words, it disturbs me to realize that I saw him only twice in my life. Better not count the third time, for by then poor Len Yu was dead and the only thing I could recognize of him was the appearance of his head, brutally severed, his dead face, recently captured in a painting that was about to be put up for auction at an important London gallery. I have always thought that this was already his inevitable destiny, long before our paths had crossed; but the idea that Len Yu himself could have been aware from the very beginning of such a macabre outcome to his life does not prevent me even now from being startled by the memory of those closed lips that now can tell me nothing, those eyes empty and fixed, whose brilliance I confess I found unforgettable on that dramatic evening in Shanghai when I first encountered him.

I worked then on the banks of the Yangtze Kwan as translator to a squad of French customs officers who looked on Chinese and British with equal suspicion. As might be imagined, that kind of work was hardly pleasing

to me, but it was neither better nor different from any
other that could in these times support a man like myself
in a city like that one, always halfway between war and fri-
volity, between extremes of misery and gross opulence. On
one particular night, a night that ever since sunset had
promised unusual heat, I was about to leave the guardhouse when I heard a clamor of shouting and pushing that
I immediately took to be a confrontation, not unusual in
those times—some Chinese boat surprised by the customs
officers with a cargo that was either suspect or totally ille-
gal. In fact, when I left the guardhouse, I made out, in the
half-dark of the dock, one of my superiors grasping the
arm of an old Chinaman who looked frail and upset,
shouting at him in French, and brandishing a revolver.
Close to them, another officer was inspecting, with more
alarm than concern, the contents of one of those bamboo
boxes in which Shanghai boatmen customarily carry mer-
chandise the length and breadth of the Yangtze. As for the
Chinaman, he was painfully trying to show his enraged
captor a wrinkled piece of paper, while he uttered as explanation the only two words of French he appeared to know:
"Médecins! Médecins chinoises!" It must have been something terrible that the poor man was carrying in that box,
for the guards seemed almost ready to execute him on the
spot, with little interest in understanding what he was trying to explain to them. I remember that, from the first
moment, I felt a mixture of outrage and compassion over
the way my superiors were treating the old man, to such an
extent that I had no hesitation in going over to help the

poor fellow defend himself. My good intentions, however, became quite troubled when I moved closer to the box and discovered that it contained half a dozen human heads carefully wrapped in linen, with a penetrating odor that led me to believe they had been preserved in formaldehyde. The second guard still hung back from inspecting those six boxes, among which were visible locks of hair clotted with blood, surfaces of parchment-like skin, and half-closed eyelids that looked as if they were about to open, in an attempt to return to life. Trying to keep calm, I tore my gaze from the box and approached the first officer, who had wrested the paper from the hands of the Chinaman and now handed it to me, ordering me to tell him immediately what it said. Then the Chinaman, who up until then seemed to me about to faint, looked pleadingly in my direction and pointed to the paper the guard had given me, again repeating his words: *"Médecins! Médecins chinoises!"*

If that scene in itself were not confusion enough, it was even worse for me when I saw that the document had nothing at all to do with the words the old man addressed to me. It was a commercial license so intricately bureaucratic that for a moment it seemed almost untranslatable. Below a smudged stamp from the office of Chiang Kai-shek's government, a vague text identified the bearer by the name of Len Yu, an antiquarian, and authorized him somewhat ambiguously to import and export antiques and work material as diverse as rice flour, ginger, and leather shields of various sizes. I looked at the old man and asked him in Mandarin what the paper had to do with the contents of the bamboo box, to which he went on repeating his excuses in French as if he had not understood me. "I'm sorry, Captain," I said to the officer who had given me the document, "but it seems to me that this man doesn't understand a word of Mandarin." At which the officer, with a look of disbelief that I was well used to, chose to thrust the barrel of his revolver into the old man's chest and went on cursing him. "Chinese pig, now you're going to tell me where you came by these heads." The old man stopped talking and gave me then a look of such helplessness as made me tremble. There was something in his face that invited me into his conspiracy, something about the whole story that told me that the man with the heads could not be a criminal but desperately needed my help if he was to get out of this situation in which, it would seem, his life hung in the balance. Then I quietly removed the barrel of the gun from the old man's breast and told the officer that the document came from the proper authorities and that, in it, one of Chiang Kai-shek's government ministers clearly declared that the man was an assistant in the Medical College of Shanghai, where the heads, legally donated by the local morgue, were to be sent for study and investigation. For a moment, I thought the officer was about to turn on me, too, but the mention of the ministers of Chiang Kai-shek had the desired effect on him. At those levels, it was too risky for any colonial authority to erode, for relatively trivial reasons, relations with the local government, which were already tense, so the officer, after

pondering a moment, ended up freeing the old man, returning his piece of paper with some distaste, and author-
izing his shipment of boxes with the instruction that he
not show his face there again. The Chinaman, who followed his words without understanding them, joined his
hands, bowed in a gesture of thanks, and hurried to re-
cover his boxes. While I watched him wrap with extreme
care every one of the heads that formed his singular cargo,
it seemed to me that the old man shot me a conspiratorial
look, a smile both ancient and benevolent, the traces of
which remained with me until his boat had lost itself in
the gloom of the river.

A few weeks later, I caught sight of him in the streets
of Kamaran, when the vision of his macabre cargo had already joined my vast catalogue of nightmares. I had made
some excuse to have a free morning and I had decided to
use it to track down in the open market of Shanghai a
supply of polyan, which would lighten my last months in
the city. In those days, polyan, for reasons I still am unable
to understand, was one of the many substances proscribed
under the sanitary code of the colonial authorities, so that
it was necessary to explore the market's labyrinthine cor-
ners and storied alleyways to acquire some of that restor-
ative balsam, whose only threat to well-being was the
fearful hangover it brought on when mixed with whiskey
or beer.

I had spent some hours rushing in vain through the
passages of the Kamaran market when a youth who looked
more than suspicious approached to tell me in English

that his master could supply me with what I wanted. Familiar over time with such encounters, I let myself be led by the youth to a kind of alley, at the end of which I could make out a bamboo curtain with a sign that advertised the buying and selling of antiques, postage stamps, and other objects that seemed very far from polyan. I was about to tell my guide that these things did not interest me, when I discovered that I was alone. From the depths of the store, the owner's voice invited me in. Resigned by now to wasting my day in all kinds of confusion, I entered with little enthusiasm.

In the soft, cushioned shadows, I could scarcely make out the face of the proprietor, who, smiling, waited for me behind his counter. At first I did not recognize him, and I almost felt the natural revulsion a tourist feels when lured to some back room through a chain of deceptions. The man, however, went on smiling as if he were an old friend, and before saying a word, he held out to me an intricately carved box, inside of which I found a most generous quantity of polyan. I said to the proprietor that I could not afford such a quantity, not even with a month's salary, but he raised his hand in a gesture that was both amicable and dismissive. "Please accept this as a gift, my friend," he finally said. "It is the least that I can do to thank you for your help that night in the port." It was only then that I recognized the Chinaman with the heads, although his clear accent and the perfection of his spoken Mandarin made me doubt for a moment that it was the same man. As if to make up for my confusion, Len Yu laughed lightly and went on: "I could not behave in any other way. In these cases, stupidity is our best defense. I am sure you will understand me, as you did that night." I didn't know quite whether to laugh with him or to take umbrage at his confession. I thought of telling him that, even so, I could not accept his gift, when the youth, once more reading my mind, explained that the cargo, which that night had been on the point of being seized by the customs officers, was worth much more than a whole boatload of polyan. It still amuses me to think that at that moment, forgetting that the story of the Shanghai doctors was in grand part my invention, I weighed the old man's words, trying to work out just how much a human head would be worth, how anyone could put a price on something like that, how much a professor of medicine or a forensics expert would have to pay a gravedigger for a supply of half a dozen severed heads. Meanwhile, the Chinaman must have thought he owed me a more detailed explanation of a business that was evidently over my head, for suddenly his face recovered its inscrutability, and he addressed me: "These, my friend, were no ordinary heads. They came from no cemetery, but from a place of execution. The price an executioner asks for these treasures is usually much higher than any cemetery custodian would ask." Then he signaled me to follow him into a tiny room through a door almost hidden by a jumble of old furniture, phonographs, and pottery. The old Chinaman lit an oil lamp that he hung in the center of the storeroom, and then I could see some twenty heads lined up almost lovingly on a shelf at the level of my

eyes. Flushed faces, grimacing lips, and eyelids that had
closed on the infinite forms of an atrocious agony. Each
one of the heads was contemplating me from a lonely out-
post of pain in which terror and loss were mixed, even if I
have to confess that, facing these heads, I did not feel the
same horror as on the dock that night, but instead a kind
of fascination brought on by the spectacle of death which
the old man was showing me, proudly and in silence,
watching me carefully by the light of the lamp, as if hoping that the very sight of his heads might induce in me
some kind of illumination. Realizing and rejoicing in the
notion that I would draw my own conclusions, my host let
me wander at length through his collection of wonders,
and finally, when he understood that my inspection was
over, he offered me a cup of tea and said something which
in some way I had already grasped some minutes before.
The head of a decapitated man, he explained, was just
about as close to eternity as anyone can be in this world. In
the seconds leading to decapitation, when all hope has
gone, a man's features, still living, take on the purest rep-
resentation of that fear of the infinite that makes us
human—not the pain, but the fear of death, as if eternity
was just about to touch them.

I remember little more of that visit to Len Yu's store,
but I was quite certain that I was in no mind to ask about
the final destination of that gallery of ghostly heads. In
some way, I was sure that those heads were not to be there
forever. Otherwise, I was troubled at not being able to recognize on the shelf a single one of the faces I had glimpsed

on the dock that night. However it was, the tea the old man had given me, his general calm, and the authority with which he addressed me kept me from asking more questions, questions I could only repeat to myself when, somewhat confused, I left the store and made for home, furnished with a supply of polyan so generous that it would have to be used a little faster than I had come to believe was acceptable.

I think I already mentioned that I never again saw the old man Len Yu, but one way or another his presence remained with me in the months following my visit to his store. First, along with my sense that the heads he had gathered in his store were not to remain there forever, I was suddenly certain that the old man was not simply an antiques dealer or an occasional collector of horrors. As I heard him in my memory, the tone of his reflections and the authority in his voice gave me rather the sense of him as a kind of sage, a guide to underworlds that were terrifying but certainly illuminating. Later, I had to add to these conclusions the deep impression he made that caused me to recognize his presence in the unlikeliest of places.

A few weeks before I was finally to leave for Europe, Michel Noel, a companion in my excesses, who had inherited a fortune and devoted himself now to dealing in art and the immoderate consumption of opium, invited me to one of those gatherings that even then took place with some pomp in the great houses of the International Settlement, as though to deny nostalgically that all this would soon end. That dinner was held in a house close to the

American embassy, and as I arrived I could not help feeling a certain revulsion at the visible bad taste of the owners, obviously clients of Noel's, who collected works of art for their market value rather than for the impression they left on the eye and the mind.

I can say little about that gathering which would not apply to many others that come back to me, like a variable ritual which mostly left me with an ungrateful sense of shared pointlessness—the dinner, the drinks, the animated groups, and the chatter which, as boring as it was forgettable, brought me once more to the point of regretting sincerely that I had come at all. Noel had disappeared with a woman of doubtful reputation, and I suppose I had decided to drown my disaffection with some drinks, when I found myself involved in a conversation that dissolved the effects of the alcohol and brought back sharply my memories of the Chinaman with the heads.

At a certain point, some of the guests had moved to the large window to look down from there on parts of the city that had been devastated by Japanese bombs. At my side I found a venerable gentleman who, as if awaking from a train of thought seemingly brought on by some of my tipsy observations, confessed to me that what I had said had reminded him of a terrible case that was still disconcerting the local police. At first, I listened to him with half an ear, trying to remember just what I had said to enliven a conversation that held little interest for me. But then the gentleman began to tell me that over the course of the last few weeks, the police had been looking without success for the perpetrators of a number of crimes committed in the most exclusive section of the International Settlement. According to him, a gang of highly trained assassins had broken into the houses of important colonial officials to commit murders of exaggerated cruelty. Most disturbing of all, according to my interlocutor, the heads of the victims had disappeared, and the general suspicion was that those who held the heads were closely connected with the Communists, especially with the Kuomintang.

No need to tell you how much that man's remarks upset me. If I found it difficult to imagine old Len Yu as a militant in the Communist Party, or bursting into a house to sever the heads of my fellow foreigners and offering them as trophies to our enemies, I could not help thinking that the old man, one way or another, was behind that business. I tried to remember my first sighting of the severed heads in the store, and although I could not remember any of them with Western faces, that did not keep me from being tempted, almost obliged, to tell the gentleman at my side how much I knew about the whole affair. I was about to do it when we were interrupted by the exploding burst of a bomb that the Japanese had dropped a little too close to the International Settlement and a general cry, more of astonishment than alarm, brought an abrupt close to the gathering, which in any case was going nowhere.

I still do not quite know what kept me from immediately denouncing the old Chinaman. From that day on, I was torn between my obligation to do so and the inexplicable conviction that that man could not be guilty of the

terrible crimes that nevertheless pointed to him with ac-
cusing insistence. Even so, my indecision was unexpectedly intruded on by Len Yu himself. One afternoon, when
I returned from a short journey to the interior in prepara-
tion for my departure, the porter at my lodgings handed
me a brief but dramatic note from the Chinaman with the
heads, written in French in an elegant handwriting. The
old man asked that I go to see him at once at his store in
Kamaran, for I had to accompany him to the police station
to make a serious charge, about which he gave no details. I
remember my surprise at seeing his signature, so careful
and elaborate compared with the urgency of the message,
a small work of art, like those that turn up in everyday acts
among Orientals. I did not think twice before answering
his summons, not because I felt bound to Len Yu by any
kind of solidarity, but because that would be my last
chance to clear up my doubts about his strange hobby and
his possible connection to the assassins in the International Settlement.

About an hour later, I arrived at the Kamaran market, after plunging fruitlessly into the bombed streets of
Shanghai and making my way through crowds that made
me think at times that Len Yu's alley had ceased to exist.
When I eventually reached the store, I had a sense of having arrived too late. The sign that advertised Len Yu's antiquarian interests hung facedown from a single nail, as
though someone had tried in vain to wrench it from the
wall. As I came closer, I felt the hostile glances of various
neighbors who appeared briefly on the street to close their

shutters in a hurry. As I feared, inside the store I was received, not by the Chinaman with the heads but by a
much younger employee, possibly the same youth who had
previously led me to Len Yu and who, on seeing me now,
seemed nervous to the point of hostility.

He did not speak French, and his dialect was so
clipped that I could not find out with any clarity about the
whereabouts of Len Yu, who, as far as I could tell, had to
be something like the boy's grandfather or a kind of distant uncle. When I showed him the note the old man had
sent me, the boy looked at me suspiciously, and after
thinking a moment, he explained to me in a low voice that
Len Yu had disappeared some days ago. Now he spoke
with a little more fluency, as if he hoped that I would be
able to help him. It was clear that he was frightened, and
was still not completely sure if he could trust me, or if the
very fact of my presence in the store was risk enough for
him. Convinced that he had nothing more to tell me, I
was on the point of leaving, when a young woman came
out of the back room. In her face, I could instantly recognize a desperation that had gone beyond any fear, a kind of
hatred mixed with an air of supplication, which frightened
me as much as the uncertainties of the boy. The woman
came close and uttered something in Chinese that I could
not understand, and then, speaking more slowly in French,
explained clumsily that her father had been taken by his
disciples. She said this with some bitterness, her words
containing both a hint of treachery and an appeal for justice to which I, still trying to put what she said in some or-

der in my mind, could only reply in monosyllables and promises which obviously I was in no position to fulfill. I was about to ask her who were those disciples she mentioned when the youth came up to her and ordered her out, at the same time begging me with a desperate gesture to leave the store immediately. I did what he asked, as afraid of his company as I was of the police, and returned home, feeling in my confusion that in some way Len Yu had cheated me, so much so that I went, that very afternoon, to file my charges in the foreign colony, but because of the war they disappeared forever in the Shanghai police archives.

We never know to what extent any sequence of misunderstandings brought on by chance will remain in the memory, any odd twist of fate or string of loose images that at first, we are sure, or we hope, are bound to be forgotten. All at once, we discover that those events in our past, seemingly insignificant, have persisted in our mind without our having done anything to retain them—objects, words, and faces that stay half-buried in the depths of our memories until, someday or other, a long time after we have registered them, an equally fortuitous event comes along that brings them back with devastating force. I am convinced by now that these surprises of remembering form part of the many deceptions of eternity, or at least that was the impression I had almost twenty years after having turned my back on Shanghai and my attempt to help old Len Yu, a vain attempt, the consequences of which I could see clearly only when it was too late for him.

At this stage, I cannot anymore remember how many months I went on suffering the winters and the drunken fogs of my drifting time in London, but they were certainly many and very long; so that when, one afternoon, I ran into Noel again, I celebrated the encounter almost as if it were a boat sent expressly to rescue me from a shipwreck. Over a considerable stretch of time, I had lost track of my envied fellow traveler from our Shanghai days, and I remember that I did all I could to hide the indignation I felt at seeing him as healthy and cheerful as in our days in the East. I know that he, too, tried to hide it, but in his friendly words and his insistent questions about my ups and downs in Europe, I was sure I could detect a hint of superiority, the unspoken boasting of someone who had committed the same blunders and mistakes as I had without paying for them with anything more than a few gray hairs, some subtle signs of bodily wear and tear, and a certain hardening about the eyes. But any humiliation I felt at his appearance was not enough to sting my pride, so that by the end of that afternoon, after some reminiscing brightened by alcohol, I agreed to help Noel sell some works of art with shadowy histories that presented difficulties on the legal market. In spite of his roguish nature, Noel proved to be a good payer, even if he seemed to take some special pleasure in the extravagance with which he treated me and made use of me. Sometimes he behaved toward me as a peer, inviting me to his parties and introducing me as his chosen disciple, but mostly he preferred to reduce me to the level of a hanger-on, and quite flatly to forget me for long periods at a time, as if he wanted to remind me of the difference between us. Our arrangement, in short, was not destined to last very long, not because of me, who at that level had little choice but to put up with things, but rather because Noel was obviously in the grip of a mercurial temperament that at any moment might make him change his mind and even his way of life.

I was not mistaken. For some days, when I was thinking that my eccentric friend had found some better assistant to carouse with and to humiliate, Noel telephoned me to tell me that he was soon leaving England and did not want to miss the chance to drink to my health and to thank me for the infinite proofs of friendship he had received from me over that period. I accepted his invitation, somewhat alarmed at my approaching orphanhood, although also hopeful that in the course of our meeting I might perhaps acquire one of those objects of value that he, driven to generosity by the demons of alcohol, used to give me from time to time to alleviate an existence that did not differ very much from the one I had lived in Shanghai.

That same afternoon, as my host seemed to be losing his composure sooner than usual, I hastened to ask him if he was thinking of disposing of his last works of art before leaving on one of his prolonged journeys. Perhaps, I added, I might be able to help him place some of these works before his departure. Hearing me, Noel was silent for a moment and then, as if he had just awakened from a long and heavy dream, his face lit up, and he confessed to me that although it was already too late to make use of my kind offer, he would like very much to show me some paintings he was thinking of putting up for auction in the coming days. So saying, he led me to the place where he kept his chosen treasures and produced half a dozen immense oil paintings of various bloody scenes from the Sino-Japanese War. More than the fires or the contorted bodies, more than the bayonets and the mud, what caught my attention were the faces of the soldiers who were slaughtering one another in those pseudo-epic paintings which, nevertheless, gave the impression of appealing to some private fear, a purely personal terror in whoever looked at them. It was then, while I was studying one of the largest pictures, that Noel spoke point-blank that arcane name the mere mention of which almost made me faint. "Len Yu," he said. "From the studio of the master Len Yu." At first I thought I had heard him wrong, as if it had been I myself and not Noel who had uttered that name I had thought forgotten. Almost immediately, however, taking my astonishment perhaps as a sign of confusion, he explained to me that these paintings were the only examples from the celebrated studio of the master painter Len Yu that the Chinese had been able to rescue from the Japanese before their defeat at Shanghai.

Twenty years had passed since the last time I learned anything about the Chinaman with the heads, and now I heard his name again as if it applied to another person altogether, not an antiques dealer, not a poor Chinese merchant left to his luck on the banks of the Yangtze, but a master, a seemingly well-known painter whose disciples had completed those enormous canvases for me alone, his version of eternity drawn from a model that only I would understand. Scarcely replying to Noel, I turned back to the paintings, and tried to recognize in each of the dying the same smoldering contortions that I had seen in the severed heads the old man had shown me in his store. I was troubled, however, to notice that these faces were not exactly Oriental ones, for immediately I could recognize in them, as in a nightmare, the funeral procession of some celebrated foreign dignitary who had received us in his mansion in Shanghai, the blond hair of an ambassador, discreetly orientalized, but, even so, disfigured now by death. In that moment, I thought that the truth about Len Yu was dawning on me with an astonishing clarity. My memory still refused to believe that the Chinaman of the heads had orchestrated the murders in the International Settlement as a sort of vengeful terrorist or a resentful artist, but I did not have the least doubt that in these oil paintings appeared likenesses of the heads that the Shanghai police had searched for in vain just before the war broke out. In a choked voice, I asked Noel who exactly were the painters in Len Yu's studio, and if he had noticed that the faces they had traced in the paintings were mainly European faces. When he heard me, Noel agreed with the excessive glee of a child whose secret game has been deciphered by its parents, and he answered that the artists who

painted these pictures had been militants in the Kuomintang, and almost all of them had been exterminated
later in Mao's cultural revolution. The master's paintings,
he added, had been destroyed during the war, but that was
not a loss to be regretted. He had heard it said that although the touch of the master was unmistakable, and
much more refined than that of his disciples, the soldiers
and the corpses that he painted were strictly Oriental, for
which reason they lacked that sinister and vengeful detail
that his disciples, in a startling display of irony and cruelty,
had added by giving their dead a secret Western look.

While I listened to Noel speaking in this way, I gave a
sigh of astonishment coupled with a vindicating relief. If
the sight of these paintings had stirred up some of my
doubts about the Chinaman with the heads, now it was
clear to me that Len Yu had had nothing to do with the
crimes in the International Settlement. At that moment, I
remembered his last message and his intention to present
his charges to the police, I heard again the voice of the
woman crying out for justice, and I had the vision, never
actually seen but always imagined, of the old man dragged
from his store by his enraged disciples and taken to his
death. I kept quiet, I went back to look at the paintings,
and then, among the contorted faces of some of the soldiers at the battle of Hum Pod, I saw the slant eyes and
the toothless mouth of Len Yu turned toward me, not in
pain but in a kind of resignation, almost as if he were on
the point of telling me that he too, after all, was on the
point of being devoured by eternity.

Time Regained

Nobody expected his death, even if it could hardly be said of Lord Gronogham that he lacked good reasons when one fine day he took leave of his servants, set fire to his plantation, and gave himself up to death, naked, on the frozen summit of Masatmala. The crew of a cargo boat that docked there some days later searched the island inch by inch for some trace—a secret formula, a grass cutting—that could justify not only their long voyage from Liverpool but their very lives. Lord Gronogham, however, had been careful to leave nothing behind him that might either confirm or perpetuate his cloudy reputation. Now his body will lie forever in the snows of the volcano, dumb, wearing guilt like a suicide's tombstone, with no God in prospect, no aid that might extract his secret, no final exhausting certainty such as comes from recognizing one's own errors too late.

For months now, his wife had written him from Rochester, regaling him with the disastrous consequences of his inflated schemes; but Lord Gronogham woke up to his responsibility only when she decided to tell him how even the paintings he so prized had begun to disintegrate on her side of the ocean. In waspish detail, she went on to explain to her husband, bluntly and unsparingly, how his favorite paintings were like shipwrecks, in galleries that seemed more and more to be cemeteries. Nobody had damaged them, she wrote. They were quite simply wearing away from being looked at so much. The oil paint cracked, slowly and irremediably, inch by inch, until eventually the most solid-appearing images came away from the canvas in tiny flakes. On the order of His Majesty, the most skilled restorers were currently busy rescuing these paint flakes. They wept over them, they preserved them in marked containers, along with a museum catalogue, out of nostalgia, who knows, or perhaps in the hope that some-one, in a better century, would be painstaking enough to reconstruct those wistful jigsaw pieces. There they all were, the sharp-leaved, bright-colored landscapes that had led Lord Gronogham to set out on his expeditions to the Pacific; and there they were, too, his languid children, his foolish-faced clowns in crimson, his fierce Venetian blues, his French greens, and his Christ figures, so many Spanish Christs who had died as he did—naked, alone, abandoned to sorrow and the cold—hoping that the plague in his body would one day be known to all men, and would com-pel them to vomit up the poison that he had invented, or discovered, for them. Poison. Even he took to calling it that as Lady Gronogham's written complaints grew more explicit. The very idea that his wondrous infusion would now go down the throats of men so inept in dealing with the long hours of night seemed ultimately intolerable to him. Opium had at least wrapped them in a worry-free trance; and cyanide had killed them, reducing the heavy weight of their empty days to one fatal moment. In contrast, his infusion mercilessly prolonged insomnia and its accompanying agonies; it brought to those who drank it an enormous serpent of empty hours that nobody ever knew how to use.

At first, when he arrived on the island and had made arrangements with neighboring farmers to single out, among the local herbs, a specific one that would reduce sleep with no ill effects, Lord Gronogham was sure he had found the closest thing to the fountain of youth. Of this he soon informed the Royal Society of the Sciences, in papers that rang with the triumphant tones of one who has grasped the Holy Grail. In short, the famous traveler announced the almost total reduction of sleeping time and, with it, the removal of the last obstacle for restoring to the civilized world a leisured, secular existence, essential for the development of the arts, the sciences, and of new ideas. Lord Gronogham's claims seemed as vague as they were definitive: a single dose was enough to reduce the habitual eight hours of sleep to two, with no physical ill effects; no prescription was needed; there was no risk of overdosing. The only sacrifice required by his infusion was a total renunciation of dreams, to be expected when extended wakefulness reduces the rest period to a kind of catatonia. Lord Gronogham offered arguments in favor of giving up dreams: it also meant giving up nightmares; and if by chance people should sense, one lethargic day, that they had lost something somehow essential, then others would set about finding the solution to that problem, given all the time available for study.

It is quite true that in all this time there were those who wanted to increase the testing period of the infusion and control its distribution; but at this level the authorities had seen in the potion their opportunity to replenish the coffers of the Empire, and it seemed to them unthinkable not to fill for other nations the thousands of orders that began to clog their laboratories. Crates would pile up every day in the seaports of the continent, since nobody then seemed able to keep the ships that delivered them from traveling much more slowly than usual, or the customary frenzy of the stevedores from giving way to an ascetic solemnity. The crates were then transported inland in carts drawn by animals that felt themselves driven by hands with little urgency, the same hands that later on would take a whole minute to reach across the counter for their bags of the reviving infusion, as a balm to their everyday existence. Duels, conversations, and games of bridge would go on for weeks, a dreamless attention could dwell for hours on a newspaper headline, swollen fingers would refuse to turn the pages of overexciting novels; winks or blows seemed to go on for centuries to the eyes of those who refused the infusion, only to find themselves one day in a terrifying sculpture garden. From morning until night, the movement of bodies began to assume the stately pace of a requiem, and pores seemed able to breathe only in the timeless atmosphere of those museums and galleries that Lady Gronogham described so gloomily in her letters.

All this time, Lord Gronogham, still insisting that the disaster was quite beyond him, decided to devote his own dead days to shaping, from the clay of the archipelago, a life-size figure of his wife, a loving rendering, promised and put off in his early days as artist without either the talent or the time to free his ambitions. Even so, the sculpture remained uncompleted, from the moment that its author discovered that he had lost not just his dreams but any control of his own impatience. Because of this, there was plenty of time not only for his art but also for his doubts and his forgetfulness, and for the alteration of forms, curves, and textures that never reached any point of conviction.

It may be true that it would have been enough for Lord Gronogham to destroy his plantations and his laboratory to slow the spreading disaster of sleeplessness he had generated overseas, but that does not mean that his immolation could have been avoided. No man in his place could ever refuse to accept the idea that when those who drank the infusion woke up from their nightmare of wakefulness, they would have to face an existence dominated once again by the certainty of death, a horizon empty of Christs and dripping clowns, the absence of which would make these onetime sleepwalkers feel they had watched an essential train pass them by that would never stop for them again.

Surely then they would think of Lord Gronogham, and
vainly curse the cowardice that drove him that morning to
strip off his clothes and wait for the cold to end his life,
while he clutched a Dürer lithograph so gray and washed-
out that it seemed already to have lost all substance.

A Note About the Author

Ignacio Padilla was born in Mexico City in 1968. He is the author of several award-winning novels and short-story collections, including *La catedral de los ahogados* and *Subterráneos*, and he won Spain's prestigious Primavera Prize for his novel *Shadow Without a Name* (Scribner, 2002). Ignacio Padilla stands at the forefront of the literary movement Crack, which seeks to relearn "lessons given to us by the great masters of the Boom."